Three Guys Talking:
My Wife or My Children's Mother?

Adeoka O. Laiyemo MD, MPH
7/20/2018

Three Guys Talking:
My Wife or My Children's Mother?

Book 1

Adeyinka O. Laiyemo, MD, MPH

ISBN-13: 978-0-9996356-1-2

Publisher's Note: The characters and events portrayed in this book are fictional and or are used fictitiously and solely the product of the author's imagination. Any similarity to real persons, living or dead, places, businesses, events or locales is purely coincidental.

Photograpy (interior and cover): Adeyinka O. Laiyemo

Editing: Ms Jamilah El-Amin
jelaminedits@gmail.com

Print Formatting: By Your Side Self-Publishing
www.ByYourSideSelfPub.com

Blissful Gardenz Inc.
P.O. Box 15581,
Alexandria, VA 22309

Email: alaiyemo.bgardenz@gmail.com

DEDICATION

This novel is dedicated to those who care about others.

ACKNOWLEDGMENTS

To the glory of the Almighty, I say a heartfelt thank you to all of you from A to Z.

I never could have and I never would have done this without you.

FROM THE AUTHOR

Thank you for your interest in this novel, a romantic seriocomic literary fiction set in modern day reality. This novel is episode one of a trilogy which chronicles the love life of three men from their points of view. Ray Marshall, Kamal Brown and Adam Gray were reunited after not seeing one another for about twenty years. They met at a neighborhood development conference which provided an opportunity for them to reconnect and they discussed their ongoing challenges in their love lives.

Ray has been married to Desiree for thirteen years, but he does not feel the joy of marriage. It appears that his loneliness worsens with each child the couple has, making him wonder whether he has a wife or a mother for his children.

Kamal had a wonderful but brief marriage to Kandie, his college sweetheart. Things fell apart due to issues surrounding having children. Kamal felt he was treated badly in the legal proceedings surrounding their divorce. He later married Bonita, who he regards as the model wife. Things took a dramatic turn when Kandie wants to get back into Kamal's life using their only child as bait.

Adam is a forty-two-year-old widower taking care of his two children for three years. He came to a proverbial fork in the road. He must decide whether to marry Nora, a twenty-year-old hottie he fell in love with and confront the myriad of challenges associated with it or marry Aneida, a thirty-nine-year-old divorcee with two children who can be a mother to his children.

Ray, Kamal and Adam discussed and offered solutions that are uncertain whether they will produce the desired results. The situations of these three friends present a conundrum: if you had to make an important choice using your heart or your brain, what would you use?

This novel is intended for those who consider themselves young, either in the mind or body or both.

For neophytes who are still trying to figure out what love means, this novel may be of help.

For newlyweds who have no idea what is in stock for them after the "I do" and the music stops, this novel may give you some insight.

For recently married couples whose straight line with their spouse has become a triangle with the children being at the opposite angle, this may help you find other angles to maintain your relationship.

For those who have been married for so long and complacency has set in, this novel may help you rejuvenate your flame or help you avoid some pitfalls.

For those mature couples who have put up with each other for so long that they have adopted a watchful waiting approach for a natural end as the best strategy, what can I tell you? Well, read it together for fun!

CONTENTS

Prologue

Yes. You know.

Yes. You know that men bleed red blood too.

Yes. You are quite aware that men have emotions too.

The problem is that men pretend a lot. They want to be seen as always keeping things in control. They want to be seen as being in charge. They convince themselves that they don't need help even when it is very obvious that they do. No matter how jelly the soft side of a man is, he still makes the futile attempt to hide his emotions. This is especially true when the issue involves women or when women are around.

However, men do talk. They just talk amongst themselves. Often in few words, but sometimes they chatter. Such was the situation at the Youth Development Conference which brought three friends together after about twenty years of losing contact with one another. They met at a conference organized by the neighborhood watch organization of the community where they grew up. The new president of the organization wanted to change neighborhood watch to neighborhood development, which uses residents—current and former—to give back to the community in terms of developing parks, community centers and mentoring the youth. It was remarkable for many former residents to walk or drive through their old neighborhood and see their old schools. The conference took place at The Magnificent Paradise Hotel in the City of Lanham in Maryland.

3

The atmosphere in the hotel was electrifying. It was amazing how things have changed in the city and how things have remained the same. Old pals who have not seen one another in decades were happy to reconnect. Old rivalries seemed rekindled and old prejudice did not die completely, especially when talking about those rivalry Friday night football games between Verdant High School and Riverdale High School. For most people, the reunion was an opportunity to rewind and bask in the glory of their achievements over the last two decades. People mingled with the crowd shaking hands with anybody who offered.

Ray, Kamal and Adam had lived in the same neighborhood and attended Verdant High School on Princess Garden Parkway. Adam is now a physician practicing in College Park, Maryland. Ray is an attorney with a law firm in Washington DC, while Kamal is a Certified Public Accountant in Old Town Alexandria in Virginia.

The three friends decided to have some refreshments together after the conference. They chose Fantastik, a new restaurant in the hotel with an international style cuisine. After talking a bit about the weather, highlighting the scorching heat of the sun in the past few days, somehow the conversations evolved into talks about their families.

"How is the family?" Adam asked.

"So-so," Kamal replied while gesturing his right hand to convey "neither here nor there," a very strange answer. It is well known that everybody says "fine" or "great" whenever such a question is asked regardless of what is going on. Then, there was an awkward silence.

Then Ray remarked, "I am not sure whether I should say that I am married, or if I should say that I am a human ATM machine for the lady in my house and her children."

Now, that took strange to another level. Ray continued that he thinks that marriage classification popularly written as married / living as married; single; widowed; divorced should be modified. He took a sip of the drink in his glass. At minimum, there should be a new class that should be "married living as single." Adam and Kamal were dumbfounded, but Ray ignored them and continued. "The best classification should probably be made to read married or single. Then single should be subdivided into single never married, divorced, and widowed. Married should be more comprehensive as marriedly married; unmarriedly married, and marriedly unmarried."

At this, Adam and Kamal laughed. But Ray was undeterred. He continued that those who are marriedly married are those who are truly married; they feel married and enjoy the benefits of being married. Those who are unmarriedly married are not married officially but they are enjoying some benefits that are enjoyed in marriage. This will be the living as married in the current classification. Whereas, those who are marriedly unmarried are those who with all intent and purposes are married officially, but they do not feel married as they do not feel fulfilled in their marriages.

"So, which class do you belong?" Kamal asked Ray.

"Definitely, marriedly unmarried," he replied. "And you?"

"I am marriedly married, but I have some issues with my former wife who happens to be my child's mother," replied Kamal.

At this, both of them turned to Adam, who was unusually quiet. "What about you?"

"I am doing okay," he replied.

"Come on!" Ray and Kamal shouted in unison.

"I am a widower," he replied. "Eva died three years ago. I am currently in a dilemma trying to choose between a twenty-year old lady that I fell in love with and a thirty-nine-year-old divorcee who loves me."

It became quite apparent that they were all having difficult times in their love lives. While they all had different challenges, the central problems were related to the choices they made and the ones they were about to make. Indeed, there is never an easy fix for a broken heart.

The Challenges of Choice

We have previously made choices
That have made or marred us
We are still going to make choices
That will make or mar us

If choosing one out of ninety-two
Is challenging, difficult and hard
Then choosing one out of the last two
Is the most challenging, the most difficult and the hardest

Part One

The Hobson's Choice:
The Story of Ray

Part One: Section One:
Serving the Community and Serving Yourself

I f you take it, then you should keep it. And if you keep it, then you should eat it," the soft angelic voice remarked. Ray recalled turning his head to the right towards the window in the break area at the back of the auditorium. He was curious to see who read his mind so accurately. He did not notice her when he arrived at the coffee break section. He had been falling asleep uncontrollably during the on-going lecture which had been, for lack of better words, painfully excruciatingly boring.

He needed a break from the boredom. He needed something sweet and something bitter. His goal was to drink coffee without cream or sugar with some pastries. However, there were too many choices of pastries giving him an *acute confusion crisis* of selecting among delicious high sugar treats including different types of muffins, strudel, cinnamon buns, donuts, and cakes. Using the silver sugar tongs, he had picked up a banana nut muffin onto his plate. After a few seconds, he changed his mind and put it back. He then took a chocolate chip muffin onto his plate. He walked across to the beverage section only to notice additional continental breakfast items consisting of bagels, small individual packs of cereal, milk, butter, and cream cheese. He took a bagel and cream cheese and walked back to the Danish pastries section to return the muffin when he heard the voice telling him not to put it back.

"I will not be contaminating the food if I put it back," he replied.

"True. But you should have weighed your options and surveyed what was available before hastily making decisions," she added.

Ray was unprepared for such a sharp criticism from a stranger, but he tried to maintain his cool. He walked towards her and noticed that she only had a few grapes on her plate and was drinking tea with the thread of the tea bag draping across the cup. His cool did not last long as he remarked, "So, if I may ask, how many minutes did it take you to decide to take the black grapes rather than the green ones?" Ray asked quite sarcastically.

She did not answer him, but she simply walked away. As Desiree turned away and headed towards the trash container to throw away her disposable plate, Ray got a glimpse of her. Something about her sparked in him. Thirteen years later, he is still riveting with nostalgia about that first encounter. Indeed, something struck him like a lightning bolt. She looked so gorgeous in her blue flowing gown with a six-inch belt loosely hanging around her waist. Her hair was covered with a head gear that reminded him of the painting of the Egyptian Cleopatra. She shot a disappointing glance at Ray, with a slight shaking of her head in disbelief at his behavior. Ray noted this demeanor, but he paid more attention to how beautiful she looked.

"She has a noticeable dimple on the right side of her cheek. Her eyes shone like gold, her teeth were as white as snow on top of a mountain, and they sparkled like a million diamonds. She looked as beautifully inviting as an ice-cream cone on a hot summer afternoon. She walked gracefully, confidence in her strides, as she returned to her seat," Ray continued.

Adam and Kamal looked at each other and chuckled.

"Wow! Did you mean that you saw all that while lowering your gaze?" Adam asked sarcastically.

"Em... em... yeah!" Ray replied, trying to fight back his laughter.

"Yeah right!" Kamal interjected. "Apparently, you can see her even if your eyes were closed!" he remarked.

"Okay, maybe I looked at her a little bit," Ray admitted while gesturing with a small space between his right thumb and his index finger. "By that time, I felt like a jerk about the way I had responded to her. I really wished that there could be a time reversal for us to have a do-over."

Ray paused for a moment. He shook his head as a faint smile streamed across his face. He was relishing in his recall of how he met his wife of thirteen years. Desiree was a sophomore at the University of Brooklyn in New York. She was studying Marketing. Ray was a law student at the University of Brooklyn's King Solomon School of Law. They were attending a college-wide Community Engagement Summit organized by the Gamma Chapter of The Human Society, a national non-profit organization which aims to reduce human sufferings. The coordinator for the event was Dr. Ibrahim, an Associate Professor of Social Work at the University of Brooklyn.

The summit was an all-day event in the summer. The goal was to create awareness of the plight of the impoverished community in the neighborhood of the university. The summit targeted "leaders of tomorrow" by inviting college students at all levels. A total of sixty-four undergraduate and postgraduate students registered for the summit. In his introduction, Dr. Ibrahim had mentioned that many of the homeless population in Brooklyn have medical, mental health and social needs.

The keynote speaker was Ms. Dana DeVita (alias Ms. Generous), the President of DeVitality. She drew examples from her own life. She related her rags to riches story from being a nurse aid to becoming an emergency room nurse, then becoming the president of a fortune five hundred company. She acknowledged all the help she got along the way from family members and strangers. She also noted that "up to a third of an average household income goes towards having a roof over our heads." "If someone loses his job, there is a good chance that his house will be foreclosed in three to six months." She recalled being taught in high school that the basic biological needs, sleep, food, shelter and companionship, are among the important things in life that makes it worth living.

"Sometimes, we do not notice the poor among us because we are arrogant. We feel that we are not just homo sapiens but homo superiors. Many of us don't even see those who serve us when in actuality, they are not our servants. How readily do you pay attention to the maid who cleans your room in the hotel or the postman who delivers your mail? We really need to pay more attention to the plight of the people around us. How often do you see a person at a street corner or traffic stop with a sign reading *Hungry, Homeless, Help*?" She asked.

"The reality is the fact that it is very common to see individuals being homeless, but an entire family being homeless is not as rare as one would hope for," she emphasized. "Well, homeless individuals are, well, homeless!" she emphasized. "They sleep wherever they get the opportunity. Few get to sleep in shelters provided by the local government or by non-governmental organizations. Most will be seen in abandoned buildings, on benches in local parks, in dirty alleys by dumpsters and on the ground in the street—especially where there are exhaust vent fans—to pass the night. Yes. America has very poor people too. It is just uncomfortable for us to recognize this."

Under Our Noses
Sometime
Many a time
A lot of time
Every time

We look at them
But we don't see them
They are in our field of vision
But we don't visualize them
They are right under our noses
But we don't notice them

Because we don't want to acknowledge them
Because we don't want them to exist
Because we see them as nuisances
Because we are afraid of them
Because we feel superior to them
Because we see them as failures
Because we just don't care enough
Because we don't think that it can happen to us
Yet, it does not take a lot
For us to be homeless too

From this powerful call-to-action speech, subsequent speakers just sounded boring. That was why Ray got up to get coffee.

The program consisted of lectures, a panel discussion and team building activities. In the afternoon session, the participants were divided into four groups which corresponded to the four cardinal points: North, South, West and East. Each group was charged with discussing and coming up with easily achievable programs to assist the neighbors of the university. The highlight of the summit was the cardinal presentation from the groups.

Yes. It is wonderful in Brooklyn, New York.

Quite fortuitously, Ray and Desiree were in the same group. All group members introduced themselves. They were asked to state their names, courses of study and anything they thought was important. This gave Ray the opportunity for him to introduce himself to Desiree. He stated his name and that he was a law student. As per what he thought was important, Ray stated, "It is important to have a second chance so that people can right their wrongs."

Since he said this looking straight at Desiree, she knew that it was a subliminal message to her while the other group members innocently felt his statement was addressing the plight of the underserved that may have been caused by the society. According to these uninformed group members, this summit was an attempt to right those wrongs.

During the group discussion, Ray tried to act mature in his approach. He chose his words carefully and was very courteous to the other participants. Although, he was dragged to the summit by his roommate, Ray now felt grateful to have come. Meeting Desiree had made it all worth it. His intention was first to get to know Desiree better and secondly, to assist the homeless. "What an honorable intention," Ray convinced himself.

Strive for Life

What is life?
If we don't get to share it
Why should we strive?
If we don't get to enjoy it
Why bring out a fife?
If we can get a band to play it
Why get into a strife?
If we can join forces
Why not get her as a wife
If you think you'll be better for it

Ray smiled at Kamal and remarked, "Thus, Desiree became my focus of attention. I was convinced that she would be a wonderful wife and an outstanding mother. Her arms would be a source of comfort. She would bring tranquility to all around her, and she would be a phenomenal pillar support for the entire family."

"Interesting! You came to that conclusion on seeing a beautiful girl twice within two hours," Kamal remarked.

"Yup!" Ray responded.

"It is incredible how men make assumptions, form impressions and take decisions when they are swept off their feet! Unfortunately, most women have no idea how much effect they can have on men," Adam regretted.

Ray continued his story. "The small breakout group session was to bring out ideas for community engagement. I was chosen as the facilitator for my group. During the deliberations, there were some interesting suggestions from the group which reflected blind enthusiasm from young minds," Ray continued.

"What kind of suggestions were those?" Kamal asked.

"A student suggested that we raise money from rich people and corporations on Wall Street and use the money to establish a homeless shelter which will be run by students. Although, it sounded great, it did not seem practicable. We were not convinced that there are many individuals or corporations that really care about poor people enough to generate adequate resources for such an endeavor. Moreover, since this will essentially be a twenty-four-hour operation, it will be impossible to run it through volunteer efforts from students who are supposed to be in school. Another suggestion we got was to start a statewide initiative referred to as the Adopt a Homeless Person Initiative, pronounced as AAHPI (Happy). In theory, this is essentially a family taking a homeless person or persons home and taking care of them. It is a very altruistic idea, but the practicability of it was very doubtful. However, Desiree suggested something on a small scale that can then be expanded. She recommended feeding the homeless in collaboration with a soup kitchen about two miles from the campus. The suggestion was well received and was upheld as being more feasible. The idea of feeding the homeless was viewed as something we can start in earnest and begin to implement in the short term and can easily be continued as a long-term community service activity. Desiree suggested feeding the homeless on the first Saturday afternoon of every month. She argued that there will be availability of adequate number of volunteers in the morning for cooking and packing the food. The food would not cost much and if everybody contributes as little as ten dollars per month, she argued that we can easily raise a thousand dollars every month for the project and have enough to provide good nutritious food for about two hundred and fifty people. We can start with two sites: at the corner Greensboro Avenue and Flatbush, and at the corner of Sterling Avenue and Midwood Lane."

For a moment, it was as if Ray travelled to a very happy place. It was clear that discussing this event brought him a vivid love memory. He had a satisfying look on his face and an indescribable smile as he recalled how Desiree presented her opinion.

Overwhelmed by Her Love
Her concern was genuine
Her interest was sincere

Her passion was palpable
Her pitch was brilliant
Her delivery was smooth
Her invitation was engrossing
Her argument was compelling
Her demeanor was captivating
Her energy was invigorating
Her tone was relaxing
Her voice was soothing

"And her lips were kissable too," Adam interjected.

This made the three of them burst into uncontrollable laughter. It was too obvious that the feelings that Ray had developed in that short time towards Desiree had melted his heart like a burning candle.

"Okay." Ray admitted. "Maybe, I was beginning to like her."

Adam and Kamal opined that it must have been her beauty that did the trick, but Ray insisted that it was her passion to help the needy. Regardless of the cause, the effect was that Ray wanted to know more about her. When the short break-out session was over, the working groups were to present their ideas for the community to the entire summit attendees. As the facilitator, Ray had to present the idea from his group's deliberations. It was a golden opportunity for Ray to engage Desiree in discussion under the pretense of working on the presentation, a strategy every smitten guy understands. After all, it was her idea to feed the homeless. He seized the moment during the tea break before the grand presentations from the four working groups.

He started with innocuous, non-probing questions like, *Do you currently volunteer, or have you previously volunteered in a homeless shelter? Are you a social work major? Where are you from? How long have you been in New York?* Sometimes, he asked questions without waiting for a response. She just shook her head and smiled.

Ray pouted his lips and then remarked, "It was all about preparing for the presentation."

"Damn right skipper," opined Kamal sarcastically.

"Yeah right," Adam remarked.

"Well, I did what I had to do." Ray convinced himself and continued, "The presentations were outstanding. The North group presented first. They were aiming for the sky. They opined that a lot of people in the neighborhood have no health insurance, particularly the homeless population in the section of Brooklyn where the University is located. A substantial percentage of the residents are below the poverty line. They argued that the area is blessed with some medical doctors working in a nearby hospital and there are many Registered Nurses and some licensed Practical Nurses. They suggested exploring having a free clinic for the indigent. They argued that if the free clinic provides a great service, we would be able to attract patients with third party payers. The emphasis would be on primary care for adults. Services could subsequently be expanded to include children. The clinic would provide basic preventive care services, such as Papanicolau smears, vaccinations such as flu shot, childhood vaccinations for school, et cetera.

The group emphasized starting on a small scale and using periodic health fairs which should feature services like blood pressure measurement, weight and height measurement for obesity screening and counseling, cholesterol check, and basic education on healthy living and healthy dietary practices. This would also bring attention to these residents by the county government. There should be a different theme every month with a health education forum which will be open to the public on the last Saturday of the month. This educational forum will be featuring a keynote speaker who will be an expert in the field of the chosen health topic. For example, we would invite the Brooklyn County Medical Officer to speak about flu vaccination in September and share important information with the residents. This information will include enlightening the residents on the activities of the county and health resources that are available for the population such as where the uninsured can obtain free vaccination or at a reduced cost. 'How cool will that be?' The presenter asked the crowd to a thundering applause. There were lots of questions about the logistics of doing this. This included how to get volunteers in all service areas, how to generate funds to pay for the staff, and where the clinic would be located."

"The South group followed the path of excellence too. Their representative, Mr. John Chan related to the summit that their group recommended a Community Empowerment through Manpower Development (CEMP) program. They argued that long term and self-sustaining improvement can only come through education and ensuring a prosperous future for the youth. This will produce a future generation of rising stars. Their overall goal was to improve the manpower and skill development of the members of the neighborhood. First step would be to secure some classrooms on campus and recruit undergraduate and graduate students to be volunteer teachers to teach middle and high school students from the neighborhood in Science, Technology, Engineering and Mathematics (STEM) related courses and language arts."

John submitted, "We can use college student volunteers as the teachers at the onset, but as the services become popular, we may ask for donations and possibly charge nominal fees for those who can afford it. The goal is to ultimately move the program as soon as possible into the community itself rather than having the students continue coming to the campus. We will need to get a facility in the community, preferably one with a recreation area such as a full basketball court or a half court due to space limitation, swings and play pen. The students will be assisted with their college applications and will be given career guidance. There will be periodic workshop for adults too. These will feature important tools like Curriculum Vitae design, English classes for non-English speaking immigrants, and seminars on how to negotiate job positions."

He climaxed his speech with, "When we assist them to stand on their feet, they will stand tall and touch the sky. Subsequently, they will be able to give a piece of the sky to the community in return."

The West group members were a funny bunch. They dubbed themselves as "The West Wing." The group members suggested the Neighborhood Buddy Project (NBP). They opined that the best way to engage our community is by respecting their rights and assisting with things that will demonstrate their concern for the community. They suggested activities such as organizing street cleaning and community beautification projects such as planting trees and flowers along the roads in the largely neglected neighborhoods.

Ray continued, "I represented the East group and presented last. Something amazing happened as I got up to go and deliver our recommendations."

"What happened?" Kamal inquired.

"Desiree wished me good luck."

"That was the amazing thing that happened?" Kamal

questioned in utmost surprise.

"Yes, it was amazing because of the way she said it," Ray replied.

Adam and Kamal looked at each other and simply shook their heads.

Ray continued. "It was as if that was all I needed. Her voice continued to echo in my head reverberating of love. It was impossible for me to get her out of my mind. I felt as if I had known her for a long time rather than just one day. I really looked forward to seeing her again. My speech was short, sweet and direct. There was clearly an advantage of being that last presenter if the audience is well engaged."

"My strategy for the task ahead was simple. The presentation was first and foremost, an audition for Desiree's love and secondly, to advocate on behalf of the homeless people."

"I started by mentioning that among the qualities of good people is that they recognize the rights of the poor in their wealth. Many of us see the poor among us and we pass by them with contempt."

"I finished my presentation by urging that we start feeding the homeless once a week for us to begin the much larger goal of alleviating the suffering of the weak. In the end, feeding the homeless was one of the two ideas selected as pilot projects. The second project was a limited scope health fair to be done about five months later in the community park. This will include health education sessions which will cover important topics such as prevention of flu, breast cancer, lung cancer and colon cancer. There will be volunteers for blood pressure measurements, obesity, diabetes, and cholesterol screening. However, my greatest achievement that day was Desiree."

"Wow!" remarked Kamal laughing hysterically.

"I really became a lot interested in feeding the homeless," Ray continued.

"Did you mean that you really became interested in seeing Desiree through a pretense of feeding the homeless?" Kamal objected.

"You are entitled to your opinion," Ray replied and continued to narrate the experience he had on the first day of feeding the homeless.

"It was a very hot Saturday afternoon," he recalled. "We

arrived at the chosen pilot site for feeding the homeless. This was at the corner of Sterling Avenue and Midwood lane. As the van carrying the goodies parked at the meeting point, people started arriving and shortly thereafter, a long queue that wound round the building has been formed. The line consisted of mainly adult men, but there were some women and children too. Desiree was quick to spring into action with the thought that the line was too long even though it was moving. The food was already pre-packed in disposable food containers with accompanying utensils. Those waiting in line picked bottled water or soda and fresh fruit as they desired. The food was rice with baked chicken. They had salad with a choice of Caesar or Ranch salad dressing. The fresh fruits choices were red delicious apples, gala apples and bananas. Desiree broke the line into two by handing food directly to people on the opposite side. This had a tremendously reduced the wait time. Desiree was graceful, calculating and dutiful. I couldn't help watching and admiring her passion. The preservation of human dignity while assisting the poor was topmost on her mind. It was really on display during this operation as she moved like a field Marshall, which ironically became her name as Desiree Marshall, her reward for marrying me."

"And her skirt?" Kamal interjected jokingly.

"Her skirt was olive green in color, not tight fitting, but still revealed a desirable derriere. Her bum reminds you of a nice-looking crossover sports utility vehicle which leaves no doubt why many babies are conceived in the back seat of a car." He then looked squarely in Kamal's face and said, "Are you happy now?"

"How did you remember this incredible detail after a million years?" Kamal asked, being quite surprised.

"Some beautiful sights are hard to imagine, but incredibly difficult to forget. Such was Desiree on this day."

"Wow!" exclaimed Adam and Kamal in unison as Ray continued to relish in his recalls.

"There was no show off that people are being fed in this event. The pictures that were taken were those of the volunteers and the food truck with care taken not to take pictures of the people that were being given the food. The pictures taken were for the community feedback and to encourage youth participation and engagement—no video recordings and no press interviews. There were minimal conversations with the people who have come for the food consisting mainly of *peace be with you, good afternoon, how are you?* and *thank you.* "Contrary to my own prejudice, it was humbling to see how orderly these homeless people were. It really touched me. We are humans after all."

This was the first time that Ray realized and confronted his own implicit bias towards the poor. In his own mind, he was fearful that the homeless people would be rowdy. How wrong he was! The people were very orderly. Nobody asked for any extra plate, nobody took more than a bottle of water or soda. Most of them left as soon as they took the food. Very few people ate the food at the distribution site. Prejudice indeed knows no bounds and he felt guilty for thinking little of the less privileged.

The feeding the homeless project started as a monthly event, but quickly became a weekly activity of the Gamma chapter of The Human Society for many years. The cost of the food was defrayed by the society and recurrent generous donations from the members of the university as well as community members. A lot of youth participated in the cooking, packaging, organizing and distributing the food. Although they could claim credit hours for community volunteering activities, this was not the intention for most of the people involved. This was purely altruism in its pristine purity. Being there had a long-lasting effect on Ray. It really had an indelible mark on how he perceives the poor and how he sees his role in the society.

He reflected on how much food is wasted here in the United States of America, when a lot of people remain hungry. He recalled buying a hot food platter in a nearby food warehouse chain at 7:55 p.m., and the attendant remarked that she was going to throw everything remaining into trash in five minutes. It sounded like a bad joke to Ray who then decided to play along. He said, "Did you mean that if I wait for five minutes, you will remove all this good food for disposal in which case I can then get it for free?" The lady chuckled. "I wish," she remarked. "Of course not! The food will be disposed into trash. If you take it while it is still in the store, you will pay full price. However, if it is now in the dumpster outside, then it is up to you," she concluded. This was a bitter pill to swallow.

Now, it made sense to him why he often sees poor people going through the trash of these chain food warehouses with hot food sections.

"Why can't they just donate the remaining food to the neighborhood food bank or give it out to the needy directly?" Adam inquired.

"I really don't know," Ray replied. "Probably because it may not be economically profitable in the eyes of the business owners and their shareholders. Maybe, they assume that people will rather stay hungry until 8 o'clock at night to get free food."

As if in a flash of light, Ray recalled asking the attendant the same question. He remembered that he was astonished to learn from the attendant that giving the food away is against the company's policy. She said that it has to do with some regulations in the book and some liability concerns which the attendant could not really explain. The law made it more sensible for companies to throw the food away than to give it out to the needy. It made no sense to Ray who just took his food and went to the checkout line at that time.

"Why would the government prefer to feed rats in the alleys than to feed hungry human beings?" It made no sense at all. The discussion with the store attendant happened only three days prior to the feeding the homeless program implementation. Now, to see many homeless people queue for food was mind boggling to say the least.

"I have not thrown any food away since then," Ray confessed to his friends. "I used to eat only the cheese portion of pizza with the toppings like many people in this environment," he remarked. "Now, I eat all the crust," he submitted.

Ray admitted to never questioning why they always throw the edges of the crust away, but now, it really was foolish and wasteful. Similarly, he has become more conscious of wasting resources and has since changed his habits, such as running water while shaving or brushing teeth, which he now regards as a huge waste of water.

Ray admitted to being quite impressed with the organizational prowess of Desiree. His heart warmed towards her and he thanked her for the suggestion that enabled the distribution to go faster. After all, the homeless would probably rather not stand around in long lines, and some who have found evening shelters have to get back to them by a certain time or risk losing their beds for the night. Therefore, anything that would make them feel bad or cause them problems must be avoided. It was really tough for him to ignore the plight of the homeless after that experience.

"Most importantly, if I was not already in love with her, that event really chiseled her love into my heart. I knew that she is the one for me. She was obviously brilliant, outspoken, and a well-organized bombshell. I really wanted her to know how I felt about her, but I did not know how to go about it. Somehow, I was afraid of coming off as a jerk again. So, I came up with a masterplan of testing the water without diving in."

"What did you do?" Adam asked with uncanny curiosity.

"I wrote a poem on a piece of paper and kept it with me. After one of the feeding the homeless sessions, I told her that I was writing a poem for a lady and that I would appreciate her opinion on the poem. She agreed to read it."

Beacon of Hope

I never knew focused clarity of vision
Until I discussed with you
I never knew the ABC of dedication
Until I worked with you
I never knew the feeling of compassion
Until I walked with you
I never knew the meaning of passion
Until I fell in love with you
I love you

"This is so nice." She remarked. "I didn't know that you write poems."

"Do you think she will like it?" I asked her.

"I am sure she will love it," she replied.

"What if it is for you?" I asked immediately, trying not to lose momentum.

"She paused for a short while. It seemed that she did not realize that it was a set up until then. She smiled and with a broken voice, she simply said *thank you* and wanted to return the paper; but I waived it off and told her that the poem was written for her and thanked her for her efforts in reaching the less privileged. I was feeling the adrenaline rush of love and the momentum of a runaway locomotive. So two days later, I sent her a card in which I had written a poem directly to her," Ray continued.

Happy to Know You

We did meet at a great event
To take care of less privileged clients
I am sorry for my temperament
But I love your maturity and judgment

I'm convinced you're God-sent
This is not out of sentiment
For your demeanor was excellent
And you've brought me a great excitement

If we are to be each other's garment
We'll be a perfect couple in complement
And we'll be in a perpetual super enjoyment
Thank you for being benevolent

"We became close afterwards," Ray opined.

"How close?" Adam asked.

"In my opinion, we were somewhere between friends and lovers. However, given how slowly ladies warm up to men, maybe it will be from friends to slightly more than friends from her perspective," Ray replied.

"At the health fair soon afterwards, the youth came together and worked tirelessly. There were information kiosks about health insurance and benefits for the poor by the students from the school of social work. We had many student volunteers in registration and referrals. We had many physicians and medical students who volunteered at the health fair. We were able to provide some dental screening as well."

"And so it was; the feeding the homeless program became a major part of my week. We were able to sustain it because of the popularity of this community engagement and generous contributions from people who opened their hearts and their wallets. I really looked forward to feeding the homeless every week."

Kamal cleared his throat in jest.

Ray then modified his statement in a direct response to Kamal's fake throat clearing. He remarked, "Okay, I looked forward to feeding the homeless while longing to see Desiree."

In reality, this was more like:

Ignoble Intention
I look forward to seeing Desiree.
I am longing to talk to Desiree.
I am eager to discuss anything with Desiree.
I am happy to catch a glimpse of Desiree.
I am motivated to be around Desiree.
I am dying to be with Desiree.
I am terribly in love with Desiree but
I am here to do something... Oh yes, feed the homeless!

After a few months, I became convinced that I had known enough about Desiree to conclude that she is the one for me. She is intelligent and very smart. She has a beautiful heart and a beautiful body to match. I added one plus one and got a million and one. I let her know my intentions by sending her a bouquet of red roses, a box of chocolate and a card in which I had written:

My Love for You
My love for you
Is more than I can qualify
My desire for you
Is more than I can quantify
My longing for you
Is more than I can justify
My affection for you
Is more than I can characterize and
My constant thinking about you
Is more than I am willing to admit
Stay blessed, my love

"Aww!" remarked Adam. "That is so nice. What did she say?"

"Honestly, I don't remember but I am sure that it was not *leave me alone*! We became closer afterwards. I was always happy to be with her and I seized every opportunity to do so."

"Like feeding the homeless?" Kamal inquired.

"What exactly is your problem?" Ray asked Kamal jokingly.

"Just wanted to keep it real, brother! An action can be judged according to the intention behind it." Kamal explained.

"Both actions are not mutually exclusive in nobility. It is noble to feed the homeless and it also noble for me to take care of myself too," Ray countered.

Ray and Desiree continued their friendship. This gradually became a courtship. They started going out on dates as if they have been joined by fate. Soon, their families became aware of the relationship. Later, Ray graduated from law school and took a job with a law firm on K Street in Washington DC. This was home coming of sorts since he grew up in Lanham in Prince Georges County, a few miles from the Nation's Capital. Before he left New York, he proposed marriage to Desiree, leaving no doubt what he has in mind.

My Mind

I sincerely hope you don't mind
That you are always on my mind
For you are gentle, nice and kind
And you are the best a man can find

Although my love for you is totally blind
I know that you are very hot, front and behind
So, let us join hands and minds
As I hereby ask for your hand, hoping you won't mind
I love you.

"Our wedding took place in Baltimore, Maryland, where Desiree's parents reside. We timed the wedding such that it would be two weeks after Desiree's graduation from the university. Prior to the wedding, the most challenging task was securing an apartment for us to reside. Obviously, I had to leave the apartment that I was sharing with a friend in preparation for my wedding. You guys know that as a bachelor you only think about yourself, which is very easy. As a married man who is in love, that is a totally different ball game. I had to consider the neighborhood, proximity to parks, grocery stores, et cetera. Those apartment rental people can really give you a big headache with their requirements. The well established high-rise apartments tend to be luxury brands costing two arms and two legs, while the affordable ones tend to be in not-so-great neighborhoods with unwanted co-tenants like roaches and rats. I saw a very affordable apartment in a somewhat good neighborhood. When I read the online review of the complex, I was mortified. As part of their advertisement, the apartment complex boasted of eliminating pests. However, a current tenant in apartment 202 contradicted the apartment managers. He related that the management only reduced roaches by fifty percent and rats by seventy-five percent in the last two years. The tenant stated that they have so many rats and roaches that it makes sense to establish a Pest Planned Parenthood to offer some contraceptives to the rats and roaches."

"In the end, I rented an affordable suite in The Choice Apartments in Silver Spring, Maryland," Ray concluded. "Shopping for needed things was an interesting experience for me also. However, the decision for the bed was the most intriguing to me. I had a great fantasy about the size of the marital bed. *Does size matter?* I often asked myself."

Size of the Marital Bed
My preference is twin
For me, that's a win-win
There is no space to roll away
In my arms, she'll always stay

Some may prefer queen
They know what they've seen
Maybe they need a little space
For their marriage to go at a steady pace

Others may opt for a king
They may not need much mingling
So long as they are okay with it
I surely have no problem with it.

No, Ray did not buy a twin bed after all. He got a queen bed instead. Well, fantasy and reality are not the same.

The wedding day finally came, and it was a blast. They were married a little over three years after they met. It was a joyous occasion. Ray got Desiree's hand in marriage, thereby fulfilling his desire. Desiree was very happy too, smiling from "Cape to Cairo." Their friends and families celebrated with them. Life was good. If you could get into Ray's mind, this is what you will hear:

Palpitation of Love

I am running on sunshine
I am swimming on sunshine
I am gliding on sunshine
I am flying on sunshine
I am dancing on sunshine
I am glowing in sunshine

"So, did you invite the homeless people from Brooklyn to your wedding?" Kamal asked jokingly. "After all, they helped you get the girl," he concluded.

Ray simply shook his head and ignored Kamal's comment.

Adam turned to Kamal and said, "Big guy, stop interrupting Ray. I am really curious to know why he defined himself as being marriedly unmarried when he seems to have married the perfect lady of his wildest dreams."

"Okay! Mum's the word," Kamal agreed and motioned his hand over his mouth as if zipping a zipper shut from left to right.

"You are right Adam. Desiree was indeed my desire, but our problem started on our wedding night," Ray replied in a voice that seems to have resigned to fate.

"What happened?" "Did you have performance issues?" "Were you firing blanks?" "Did your soldiers run away from the battlefield?" Adam asked many questions in close succession without waiting for a response from Ray.

Ray simply shook his head in negation.

Part One: Section Two:
Progress in the Reverse Direction

After the merriments and dancing celebrations, the couple left for their apartment. They dumped whatever they could carry into the living room without going back to the car for the rest. Obviously, those could wait until tomorrow. They have both wanted to make their wedding night the first time out. Both believed that *virgin* is not a word that should be reserved for olive oil. Alas! The magic moment is here. The long-awaited moment. The moment of truth. The intimate moment.

Intimate Moments
Intimate moments
Sacred moments
You call them forbidden enjoyments

Intimate moments
Bonding moments
You wish the bonding lasts longer

Intimate moments
Thinking moments
You never remember what you thought about

Intimate moments
Sharing moments
You share something you are happy to share

Intimate moments
Caring moments
You are never sure who the caregiver was

Intimate moments
Loving moments
You think you made love or gave love

Intimate moments
Doing moments
You know what you did

Intimate moments
Rewarding moments
You get your prize in nine months

Intimate moments
Listening moments
You hear your heart beating fast

Intimate moments
Talking moments
You talk in words but not in clear speech

Intimate moments
Taking moments
You can't quantify what you took

Intimate moments
Nourishing moments
You get cooling from sweating

Intimate moments
Relaxing moments
You get relaxation by contracting your muscles

Intimate moments
Giving moments
You give stuff you never want back

Intimate moments
Worshipping moments
You get your recompense for doing it right

Ray was ecstatic. He mused to himself, "The long-awaited day has come and the night to remember is finally here." After they settled down in the apartment, they walked lovingly into the bedroom. Ray looked at Desiree. She was indeed the most beautiful lady in the world. He held her hand and she said, "There is something I need to tell you."

"Yes, baby. I am listening," replied Ray.

It is debatable if he was really listening, as he was holding her hands and pulling her closer to his chest with an unbelievable *my prayer has been answered* arousal.

"I am on my period," Desiree revealed.

"What period?" Ray asked, and suddenly he realized that she meant her menstrual period, and the implication of this made him freeze. He is not going to savor the juice of the forbidden fruit until her period is over. Immediately, he had mixed emotions of disbelief, confusion, and shock. This rapidly degenerated to disappointment and anger in a matter of seconds. Ray added one plus one in his mind and got one million with the thought that Desiree may be one of those women who keep important secrets from their husbands like he had seen on The Jerry Springer Show. This annoyed him even more.

"And you knew this all day and you did not say anything?" he shouted while trying, quite unsuccessfully, to calm down.

"It started last night," she tried to explain.

This only infuriated Ray even more and he replied, "So you knew this all day and you did not say anything?" he reiterated. The tone of his voice showed that he could not control his anger.

At this point, she withdrew from him and asked in a relatively calm tone, "What did you want me to do? You know as well as I do that I can't stop myself from menstruating."

"This is not about your period. This is about your lack of

31

adequate communication of something this important," Ray shouted.

"Why should I be telling you something so personal when you were not yet my husband," she argued.

"At least you could have given me a hint that there will be nothing tonight," Ray countered. "This was supposed to be our special night. Now it is worse than an ordinary night. We are arguing on our wedding night!" he submitted.

A Night of Nightmares

It was supposed to be a special night
An extraordinary night
A night of blissful joy
A night of release of inhibition
A night of eating the forbidden fruit
A night of delightful passion
A night that lasts forever

Now, it is a nightmare
It is a night of disappointment
It is a night of sadness
It is a night of dashed expectation
It is a night to forget.

Desiree could not hide her profound disappointment too. This reaction from Ray was shocking and unexpected. It was too bad. "This is a natural phenomenon and I am not going to menstruate forever," she said to herself. She walked back to the living room wondering what kind of a selfish and unreasonable man she has just married! *How could he not understand that things do happen that can change perfect plans? What will he do if he plans a perfect outdoor program for months only for a tornado or torrential rainfall or an earthquake to occur at the site of the event?* She continued to ask herself many questions without answers as her anger started building up in geometric progression too.

As far as she was concerned, he had behaved as if the world had come to an end. She knew that her period lasts for only five days, so it would be completely over in the next four days. She also subtracted one from one million in her mind and got zero. She wondered if Ray had married her only for her treasures down below. This thought annoyed her even more and she walked back to the bedroom door. Ray was still dazed from realizing what just went down or rather, what was not going to go down.

"I thought you were telling the truth when you said that you were marring me because you love me?" she snarled at him.

"I love you like no man has ever loved any woman in the history of mankind! That is why it is painfully disappointing that you did not give me a hint. Saying I love you is using words for expression, making love is the real deal that proves the love between the couple," Ray emphasized.

After a few minutes of awkward silence, Ray looked at Desiree and made a fence-mending remark, "You look smashingly beautiful in your dress. It is totally worthy of every penny spent on it."

Desiree forced a smile in appreciation.

Unfortunately, Ray wasn't done. He continued, "You are so attractive and inviting but you are like an exquisitely polished diamond behind a glass on display with a sign that reads *Don't touch the glass*."

Desiree became disappointed again.

It was indeed a very long day, and the night was not comforting either. In the end, both of them just got tired and retired to bed knowing that they had to pack their bags in the morning for their afternoon flight to Puerto Rico for their honeymoon. They slept on the queen size bed, but not in the position that Ray had envisaged. He faced east and Desiree faced west. For the first time, Ray wished he had bought a King size bed. He felt that he needed that space. *Why do you want to be close to a woman you can't touch?* he asked himself.

As he was beginning to fall asleep and voyaged into slumberland, he remained apprehensive. He wondered what the next day would bring. "Tomorrow morning is the beginning of a new day, the day of a new beginning," he mused to himself.

Eventually, morning came heralded by the glorious golden rays from the sun in its splendor. The cock doesn't crow in Silver Spring. Chicken are in deep fryers, not on the street. Ray did not feel refreshed at all. He still did not know how best to handle what happened the previous night. This was not one of the topics that had been brought up during their pre-marital counseling sessions. Ray became pre-occupied with what to say if his family and friends were to tease him and crack any stupid wedding night jokes, as this would be terribly distasteful. He remembered having participated in those newlywed jokes before. Now, he realized that it was not something good to do. "Those busybodies who want to put their noses in the matrimonial affairs of others should have their noses chopped off," he opined.

He knew that the best course of action is not to say anything but smile and take whatever joke was thrown at him as payback. It will always be his duty to protect his wife. Therefore, he put on an Oscar-winning performance while answering those numerous just-checking-on-you phone calls. These phone calls also made him realize one important thing; it is not a good idea to be calling a newlywed couple the morning after their marriage. In fact, it is a terribly horrible idea. In his own case, he was not able to do what he would have loved to be doing. Nonetheless, he could imagine how annoyed he would be if he was really busy getting to know his wife in the way he wanted to know her, and all these stupid, annoying, and unnecessary phone calls were coming in.

Ray looked at Kamal and remarked, "Imagine somebody calling in the morning after the wedding and he asks you if you were a real dude last night and you replied that nothing happened. He is going to quickly hang up the phone saying that he is sorry for your predicament. However, in his mind he is never going to think of you as a real dude anymore, but as a dude without the *e*. So, it is…"

"What is a dude without the *e*?" Adam asked interrupting Ray while trying to process the information. "Never mind, I got it," Adam remarked after he understood what Ray meant.

"I quite understand what you mean. No man wants to go from being a real dude to being called a dud in twenty-four hours," Kamal opined.

Therefore, Ray did his best and did not give any insight to anybody that things did not go well on their first night. After all, protecting a wife's interest and never shaming her is a quality of a good husband. Yeah! Even though it was a night to forget, Ray behaved as if everything was okay. The only exception was with the person who should matter the most, his wife. In essence, he screwed up right at the gate of their marriage because he did not get to screw.

The flight to Puerto Rico was quite uneventful. It was a trip outside the United States that is considered to be a trip within the United States. Therefore, there were no difficulties with checking in and out, border and customs issues, or dealing with drastically different time zones. The relationship between Ray and Desiree gradually improved. Although, holding hands and small love talks can be a soothing balm for a bruised ego, it was obvious that this was not the honeymoon both had hoped for. Despite the fantastic weather in San Juan and the beautiful beaches, Ray stayed indoors most of the time during the first three days of arriving for their honeymoon. He preferred to watch the television instead. Ray flipped through the one hundred and twenty-five channels over and over again without actually watching anything. Eventually, the fourth day came. It was awkward at first, but they got through it together. It was worth the wait. Ray felt released from his bondage, but Desiree never really understood why this was so much of a big deal to her husband.

She summoned the courage to ask him during a rest period between the sheets. "Why did you make so much mountain out of this molehill?" she inquired.

"My dear, it is not a molehill. It is really a big mountain, bigger and taller than Mount Everest. It is a guy thing," he replied trying to catch his breath.

"Are you trying to say that I can't understand it because I am not a man?" she wondered.

"In a way, yes," he replied. The feeling is not the same for a man as compared to a woman and the need for it is different too. It is biology driven by hormones and I believe it is only clear if one has had the first-hand experience of it."

"I don't think it is so complicated that women will not understand how men feel about it," she countered.

"It is not about how complicated it is. In fact, it is very simple and straight forward. It is a kick and start, pull the trigger and fire the weapon kind of a thing. Nothing complicated at all. The challenge is not the act itself, but it is about understanding the differences between men and women in the intensity and the feeling they have regarding it. I really think women absolutely need to understand the significance of this for an enduring relationship. Let us look at it this way. I know that very often, people think about mismatched comparison as comparing apples and oranges. If you have never seen nor tasted an apple or an orange before, you could still imagine that apples versus oranges comparisons are far off. This is because you can say apples are spelled differently from oranges and use your imagination as per how they are different. In the subject matter that we are discussing, it will be like comparing apples and pineapples. If you have never seen nor tasted an apple or a pineapple before, you are bound to think that apples and pineapples are related. It will be easy to imagine that pineapples are just apples with some pines. However, you and I know that apples and pineapples are not remotely close in comparison at all whether in size, shape, color or taste. So, my dear, apple is a fruit, and pineapple is a fruit. That is the end of the similarity when it comes to that feeling for a man in comparison to a woman," Ray concluded.

"Interesting," Desiree remarked.

"I am sorry for over-reacting and being cranky in the last few days. I hope you understand," Ray stated. She nodded in affirmation, but future events did not support such understanding and willingness to accept what Ray was trying to explain.

A beautiful beach in San Juan where Ray did not go until after four days.

After three weeks of holiday, Ray returned to work. The honeymoon was over. Desiree was sending out applications trying to join the labor force. One bright Saturday morning, Desiree felt sick and was vomiting frequently. She remained nauseous for most part of the day and it then struck her that her period was late. Ray was excited and quickly went to get a pregnancy test kit from the neighborhood Bestway pharmacy. Not particularly sure which one to buy, he read the labels and got the one that claimed to be ninety-nine percent accurate and rushed home. Alas! The pregnancy test was positive. Ray was ecstatic.

He looked at Adam and recalled. "I was so happy. I was going to be a father. Around the house, I would walk fast, then quickly slow down so as not to show my excitement. It was almost like doing the hop, skip, and jump of a triple jump sport event. It was a great feeling. Unfortunately, it was the beginning of another problem."

"What happened?" Adam inquired.

"Desiree metamorphosed and became Misses No and Lady Leave-Me-Alone to every love advance. It was really frustrating. She looked wonderful to me. Yes, she might have vomited a couple of times in the morning and was mainly taking soups and crackers, but after she took a shower, she looked even better than the knockout that she was when I first met her. Unfortunately, I was not on her mind at all. It was as if I did something bad against her. She did not want to be near me. Initially, I tried to understand that it was the pregnancy hormone thing, but it just persisted to the point that I started getting a feeling that she was just using pregnancy as an excuse and we started arguing and fighting all over again. The day I lost my cool was when she accused me of being inconsiderate. We had not had anything in two weeks. I told her that this was an eternity, but she wouldn't listen. My head was all jacked up. I went to the living room, but I couldn't remember why I went there. So I left for the kitchen, and by the time I got there, I had forgotten why I went there too. I opened the fridge, but even though it was filled with a lot of goodies that I had bought hoping that Desiree would eat something, I still couldn't set my mind on anything. So I went back to the bedroom where she had covered herself with the bed sheet and I yelled at her in a soft voice…"

"I am confused here. How do you yell in a soft voice?" Adam interjected.

"Well, when we later discussed this, Desiree claimed that I was yelling at her, but I know that I spoke in a soft voice," Ray explained.

"Yeah right! Soft voice indeed!" Kamal remarked with tongue in cheek.

Ray continued, "Anyway, I made it clear to her that the *you can't touch this* that she is forcing down my throat was unreasonable, unfair, and was making me miserable. Then I left the bedroom for the living room again. When I got there, I sat down on the sofa for about three seconds and went back to the bedroom. This time she had covered her head with the bed sheet so that I couldn't see her face. I was very convinced and absolutely sure that she must have been laughing at me under those stupid covers. Nonetheless, I told her again in a soft voice that her acts were terrible and they were making me very angry."

"And what did she say?" Kamal inquired.

"She did not respond at all, even though she was not asleep," Ray replied. At that point, I just left the house and slammed the door."

"That is really unfortunate," Adam remarked. "It is what I term to be the Early Pregnancy Paradox, or EPP for short."

"What is that, Doc?" Kamal inquired.

"It is a phenomenon that tends to occur when a lady is just pregnant. Although, she feels miserable with the pregnancy-related nausea and vomiting, the so-called hyperemesis gravidarum, but she actually looks really attractive when she freshens up. Her breasts in the front yard will be getting bigger and her derriere will be getting smoother and more inviting in the back yard. Realize that at this point, she has not really gained much weight and all the swelling everywhere has not set in. So, she is looking really hot to the husband who then cannot help himself and would want more love action. However, she is feeling sick and miserable. Therefore, she cannot comprehend why he does not understand that that is not the time for such," Adam explained.

"What then is the solution for this impasse?" Ray asked.

"I don't know. I guess if women are aware of EPP, maybe they will understand that asking the husband to be gentle in the act rather than rejecting him is the easier solution," Adam remarked. "It is more detrimental to leave their husbands on ice at any time, especially in a situation like that. The fact is that love will be erupting in his system like a volcano that is ready to release the hot molten magma in its core."

"I agree with you," Kamal added. "Ladies generally make

the blunder of saying that when a man is in the mood, fifty percent of his brain is gone."

"Of course, that is an incorrect statement. However, we have to realize that they do not have any insight into the issue at all. Otherwise, they will know that it is not fifty percent of his brain that is gone, it is ninety-nine percent of his brain that is gone," Ray clarified.

"How will any sensible wife maltreat her husband when ninety-nine percent of his brain has shut down, and expect him to be reasonable?" Adam asked rhetorically.

No Turning Back
If a man is in the mood
Nothing matters except his manhood
When he is standing up
Then he is truly really up
If he wants the beat to go on
All that matters is for the show to go on

"Anyway," Ray continued, the day Patricia was born was an exciting day for my family. She looked so cute and so innocent. At least, that was what I thought back then until she and her other siblings started showing their true colors.

"Now, I am confused," Adam stated. "Do you have issues with your little kids also?" he asked Ray.

"Well, I have four children and they are all driving me nuts with their mother. They are Patricia the parasite, Paige the pest, Bryan the blood sucker, and Lisa the leech," Ray surmised.

"Wow!" Kamal and Adam shouted in unison.

"What is going on man?" Kamal inquired breaking his code of silence.

"It is terrible and unfair!" Ray complained. "When we were expecting Patricia, Desiree convinced me to buy anything with *baby* affixed to it. I mean, I bought everything from baby cot, play pen, diapers, toys, you name it. I drew the line and said a big *NO* when she suggested that we should consider buying life insurance for a baby that was not even born yet! Anyway, Patricia was born, and she came home two days later. Now, I could understand the baby sleeping on our bed the first week and maximum of two weeks, but six weeks later, she was still sleeping on our bed between me and Desiree. One day, I got fed up and I confronted Desiree in a very nice and soft manner."

"Why is the baby separating us?" I asked Desiree.

"What did you mean by that?" Desiree responded with a question.

"Patricia has been sleeping between us since she was born. What is up with that?" Ray explained his point.

"Oh, I see. I need her to be close to me. This way, if she wakes up at night and needs my attention, it will be easier for me to attend to her," Desiree answered.

"I think she should be in her own bed in her own room. We will put the baby monitor on. If she cries in her room, you can hear her then go attend to her. You should then come back to our bed when you finish," Ray recommended.

"But she is too young to be by herself," Desiree pointed out.

"No, I am sure she is old enough. The obstetrician already discharged you from postnatal care and the pediatrician has discharged her from neonatal care also. I am sure that we can follow their expert opinions and we can discharge her from our bed too," Ray suggested.

"No. I will not feel comfortable with that," Desiree voiced her concern.

"Okay. As a compromise, we can rearrange our sleeping arrangement. From right to left, it will be you, me and the baby. This way, the baby still stays on our bed but not in between us," Ray explained.

"No. That will put the baby behind you. I am afraid that you may roll over the baby when you are sleeping soundly," Desiree stated being somewhat apprehensive.

"There is no chance of that happening. However, if that is your concern, the baby can be next to you. So, it will be me, you, and the baby so long as she is not between us," Ray compromised.

"But she can fall off the bed if she rolls," Desiree disagreed shaking her head.

"C'mon Desiree! This baby has not moved anywhere since she has been sleeping between us. It is like… she is a wall of some sort, just creating a barrier to our interaction," Ray complained.

"I don't think the baby is old enough to be moved now," Desiree was adamant.

Ray looked at his friends and shrugged his shoulders. "Well, guys, I couldn't make her change her mind. So, this parasite of a baby continued to limit my access to my wife. About a month later when she was now two months and about two weeks old, I was totally frustrated. I couldn't take it anymore. You know, it was as if the baby knew something was going on. Every time, I wanted Desiree and me to dance to the silent drums, this jealous baby would be crying as if she had never eaten a meal in her entire life. So, happily I must say, Desiree would pick her up to breast feed until I was either tired of waiting or fell asleep in anger. I am sure that in Desiree's mind, she probably felt that she had been saved by the baby bell. I am convinced that she trained that little girl to know precisely when to cry so that she could get out of rocking me to the beat. I am really sure of that."

"Wow!" Adam remarked. "Are you really serious?"

Ray did not respond to Adam's question. Rather, he continued his painful narration. "One fateful Friday night, this rubbish routine started again. This time, I was determined to put an end to this monkey business. So, I waited. I sat down on the bed watching both of them in their mischievous behavior. She fed her from the left breast, then the right breast. I just stood there making eye contact with Desiree and didn't utter a word. I am sure that she got a sense that something major was going down. After a very long time, the baby was already sleeping with her mouth on the breast. So, I told her that the baby is sleeping. To my surprise, she took the baby from the right breast and tried putting her on the left breast again in an attempt to wake the baby up in style. So, I shouted in a very calm voice asking her, "Why are you trying to wake the baby up?"

"I just wanted to make sure that she has had enough," she replied.

"Of course, you shouted in a very calm voice," Kamal remarked in jest.

"That is your problem. I am very sure that I spoke softly," Ray responded and continued his story. "I knew she was stretching the truth. Therefore, I remarked that I may not know anything about breast feeding, but by the time you are sleeping while eating, it does not matter whether you are a neonate or an old cargo, you have had enough food. She couldn't argue against this."

"I still have to burp the baby," she emphasized while putting the baby on her left shoulder.

"I knew that I was witnessing nothing but well-orchestrated delay tactics, but I was ready for it that day. Therefore, after another eternity, I said that if the baby has any air to belch, she would have done so by now. Desiree had no defense for my argument. So, she put the baby down in the middle of our bed again. At this point, I insisted that the baby sleeps in her baby cot in the baby's room."

"Why did we waste so much money buying all this stuff for the baby if she is never going to sleep in the cot?" I asked rhetorically.

"She is still too young to sleep by herself in a cot," Desiree replied.

"Absolutely not!" I countered. "Baby cots are for babies. She is definitely old enough." So, I put on the baby monitor equipment and picked the baby up to go and put her in her cot in her room. To my surprise, Desiree objected. After a few minutes of argument, we reached a compromise. So, I brought the cot from the baby's room to our room so that she can sleep in her cot but in our room."

"I guess that was a workable compromise," Adam remarked.

"You would not believe this. As soon as I put the baby in her cot, she woke up and started crying. If I had not been the one who put her in the cot, it would have been impossible to convince me that Desiree did not sabotage the moment by deliberately waking Patricia up. I was so angry that I just left her in the cot. Of course, her mother quickly ran to the cot to pick her up. She put her on her shoulder and started petting her for another eternity. I am still convinced that her effort to make her fall asleep was really half-witted. After a protracted petting and singing lullaby for the baby, Desiree realized that I was pretty determined too."

"I will need to check her diaper in case it is wet, so that I can change it," she informed me.

"Go ahead," I replied in a calm voice to reassure her that I am waiting and that I have no intention or plan to change my mind. She normally changes the baby's diaper in our bedroom but this great midnight, she chose to take the baby to the bathroom to check her diaper. I sat at the edge of the bed and waited. I thought that I caught her prying into the bedroom to see if I was lying down on the bed, but she realized that I meant business. So, after another eternity, she came back to the room and the baby was

42

sleeping. She then put the baby in her cot where she slept through whatever was remaining of the night. I did not bother to ask her why checking a diaper and even changing a diaper would take an inordinate amount of time, I couldn't care. As far as I was concerned, this buffoonery had to end that night."

"The vulture is really a patient bird," Kamal chuckled.

"The challenge was that Paige was born precisely nine months later in March just like his sister," Ray lamented.

Kamal and Adam burst into an uncontrollable laughter. Ray initially frowned, but later joined in the laughter as he could not help himself.

"So, you have artificial unidentical twins!" Kamal said in jest.

"Paige was born on the seventeenth day of March and Patricia was born on the nineteenth day of March. I had joked that time that Desiree should have just held on for two more days so that if they were born on the same day, at least we can do joint birthdays for both of them every year. Anyway, Desiree did not think that my joke was funny at all," Ray continued.

"Paige was a really mean pest. That little boy cried all day long. He cried for no reason. He cried when he wanted to sleep rather than just simply closing those big eyes of his. He cried when he woke up. He cried when he wanted to eat. He cried after he'd eaten. He was always holding the mother's dress. He was a truly annoying crybaby. He was a handful. Sometimes, I wish we could just put him up for adoption. Unfortunately, you can't return a baby to customer service because you don't want the baby anymore unlike what people do after the Thanksgiving holiday when they return unwanted items. Otherwise, Paige would have been an ideal candidate for being returned to wherever his mother got him from. The only good thing about him though, he slept throughout the night. He almost never wakes up at night. After making everybody miserable throughout the day, I guess he would always be too tired at night. He slept at night and would wake up the following day to torment everybody all over again. Bryan was born about two and a half years after Paige."

"Slow down skipper," Kamal interjected. "Did you mean that you have three kids in less than four years?"

"Yes," replied Ray.

"But that would be enough to drive any woman to the end of the earth," Kamal opined.

"No," Ray disagreed. "Desiree is a homemaker and I help at home too."

"How often do you really help and what exactly do you do?" Kamal inquired.

"I take out the trash when asked to do so," Ray explained with pride.

"Em... em... That is your great idea of helping out at home?" Kamal queried.

"That is not all that I do. I also sometimes make breakfast on the weekends. It is not as if I could breastfeed those babies for her anyway," Ray remarked becoming defensive.

"My friend, I am not criticizing you. I was just wondering if she was overwhelmed with those little gamma Rays she gave birth to for you," Kamal joked.

Ray was not amused. Nonetheless, he continued. "I actually liked Bryan. He was easy going unlike his brother who was nothing but a pest when he was much younger. However, I noticed something crazy when Bryan was about four months old. Every time he is suckling, he will hold on to the other breast. Initially, I thought that it was my imagination. At this point Desiree has lost interest in any hanky-panky. She definitely preferred her kids over me."

"*Her* kids?" Kamal asked.

Ray simply ignored him and continued. "It was as if she was punishing me for those babies. You know, it was like you brought them here, they take your time... em... em... kind of a deal. Every time, I complained that I wasn't getting her attention. She would reply, 'You are a grown man. You can take care of yourself. These kids need me,'" Ray explained, mocking a female voice.

Adam and Kamal looked at each other and tried not to laugh.

"Like I was saying earlier, I became convinced that Bryan was nothing but a blood sucker because of his mocking while suckling behavior. I am very serious. When that little brat is sucking the left breast, he will hold on to the right breast. I know that he was mocking me saying to himself, "I can have it and you can't!""

"C'mon, Ray," Adam interrupted. "A four-month-old baby cannot process information like that."

"I think this little one did. Maybe his mother taught him to do so. I could see it in his eyes," Ray concluded.

"I think you were just having paranoia because your love

tank was always full," Adam remarked.

"You can believe whatever you want. At that point, I made up my mind and I told Desiree that we were done with having kids and she agreed. We kept it that way until two years later when Lisa was born," Ray recalled. He shook his head as if he did not know where the baby came from.

Kamal and Adam looked at each other and chuckled.

"How did that happen?" Kamal asked Ray with a fake facial expression of surprise.

"You know it is really difficult to say no to a beautiful lady in a transparent night gown," Ray explained.

"I see," Kamal voiced understanding while laughing.

"What about Lisa, your little girl?" Adam chimed in sarcastically.

"Actually, Lisa is daddy's darling little girl," Ray replied with a smile on his face.

"I don't get this. Did you just say that Lisa is your darling little girl?" Kamal interjected.

"Yes," Ray responded.

"I thought you called her a leech just now," Kamal reminded him.

"Yeah! I did because she is still sucking time away from me like her other more virulent and peskier siblings," Ray explained.

"Now I get your disordered thinking. You are blaming your kids for the lack of attention from their mother," Kamal suggested.

"Well, if you put it that way, you will make it sound as if I am unreasonable," Ray countered.

"Don't you want Desiree to attend to your children?" Adam asked Ray.

"I am not saying that she should not attend to them. My point is that it should not be at my expense. Think about it. How much time do you really think I need from her per day? Maybe thirty minutes? One hour? Two hours maximum? I just need a few minutes during waking hours and all the remaining time is for us to unwind together," Ray explained his point.

"What exactly do you want from her? Remember that she is not Superwoman too. She would have been very busy all day long taking care of your little gamma rays," Kamal opined.

"I do not think I am asking her for too much. A smile when I get home will always be appreciated, and I will feel safe that I am where I can rest. Being asked how my day was will definitely make me happy that somebody really cares about my well-being. My boss at work doesn't give a hoot about me; he just cares about the dollar sign. Coming home to my loving wife asking me how my day went will make me forget whatever I had to put up with at work. It really makes a big difference," Ray reiterated.

"What if there are still issues to take care of? For example, if the children need to eat," Kamal inquired.

"She can give them food about an hour before I close from work or better still, we can all have dinner together to improve bonding," Ray replied.

"What if a child needs to use the bathroom during Ray's protected time?" Kamal asked sarcastically making commas air quotes with his fingers while describing the dedicated time for Ray.

"I know that you are being sarcastic, but the fact is that these children are all potty trained and if they were not, isn't that why I buy diapers?" Ray countered. "I really don't think that the children should take all the time away from me. We need time to connect."

"I am pretty sure the connections you had is what brought about four children in less than six years," Kamal pointed out.

"My friend, I am not complaining about the number of children. There are many ways to avoid children if it is an utmost priority, but don't tell me to be celibate as a married man," Ray retorted.

After a few seconds of pause, Ray looked at Kamal and asked, "So how much did Desiree pay you for this interrogation since you seemed to be on her side?"

"I will send her the bill later so that she can pass it on to you for prompt settlement. My man, I am just trying to see things from your wife's perspectives," Kamal explained with a smile.

"Honestly, I think she just used me to have her babies. All she wanted was a good father for her kids. I mean, it was ridiculous. I wasn't getting anything from her," Ray lamented.

"But you have four children," Kamal reminded him.

"C'mon big guy! It is not how frequently you do it that determines how many children you will have," Ray remarked. Since we got married, maybe four times a week at the peak frequency, which was not even enough back then. Later, it went down to maybe once in two to three weeks. She was constantly

46

saying *no, no, no, no,* as if that is the only word she knew.

On the Road of Life

The destination is happily ever after
The husband is the driver
The wife is the road owner

If she makes things smooth and easy
His head will be clear and not fuzzy
The drive will be an enduring bliss

Yes, she grants access to the road
But she did already when she said, "I do"
Why now make things unnecessarily difficult?
Why create an environment that causes faults?

If she puts a speed bump
It makes him behave like a bum

If she puts a stop sign
It is annoying and makes him sigh

If she puts a toll gate
It makes him resign to fate

If she puts a road close
It breaks him and they stop being close.

To your husband, do not say no
To wise women, this is a no-no.

Ray related that he complained bitterly. He and Desiree later agreed to seek mediation. He asked her to check with her primary doctor to run some tests in case she was having hormonal failure of some sort, but her results were all normal. Later she suggested that they go and seek help from our respected elder and minister. They did and after he heard them, he explained to her that it is not a good thing for her to be denying her husband.

"Sir, he wants it every day. Sometimes more than twice a day especially on some weekends," Desiree countered.

47

"That is very healthy. I would have thought that you would be happy. It only shows that I love you and I want to be with you," Ray responded.

"Why so many times? I mean, this is not food!" Desiree shouted.

"Well, if you think of it as a bosom sandwich when the legs are the bread, then it will sound like food. Believe me, no man will choose any food over a bosom sandwich," Ray explained in a jovial manner trying to diffuse the tension.

"I think you just lack self-control," Desiree remarked pointing an accusatory finger at Ray.

"I lack self-control? Are you kidding me? Self-control in this regard is for those who are not married. Why did we get married in the first place?" Ray asked her.

"I thought you said that you married me because you love me," Desiree reminded him.

"Exactly my point. I am calling you for us to make ____," Ray paused, opening is hands in anticipation of Desiree completing the statement with the missing word.

However, she did not complete the statement, but rather she rolled her eyeballs like teenagers often do when they realize that they lost an argument.

"At this point, the minister weighed in," Ray continued. "He advised that she should try her best and accommodate my needs. However, my wife felt that the minister was just supporting me as a man rather than looking out for her. I still think that her statement was ludicrous. Desiree claimed that we live in a biased patriarch system, especially in religious institutions. I disagreed. My argument to her was that firstly, she picked the clergyman. Secondly, he is a man. Therefore, he understands issues with a man's needs. If we were talking about menstruation, I asked, "Don't you think a woman will give a better answer based on her understanding?" Rather than showing understanding, she snarled at me accusing me of sexism. I still think she was unreasonable, and her comment was totally absurd. The need for intimacy is different for a man than for a woman. What do we have to do to make women understand this simple fact?" he asked Adam and Kamal as he threw his hands in the air in utter disbelief.

"Things just degenerated," he continued. "Anytime, she realizes that I am going to ask for her attention, she will suddenly develop this so-called headache. It was as if there is a school where all women are taught to develop headaches when their husbands are seeking their pleasure. Sometimes, she will just stay in the kitchen pretending to be busy. There was a particular day that she was putting on her show of shame as usual. That day, I decided to monitor what she was doing in the kitchen at eleven thirty in the evening. I guessed that she was hoping that I would be asleep before she came back to the bedroom. After watching her just sitting down in the kitchen for about ten minutes, I confronted her. She gave me the most bogus excuse any man has ever heard. Bear in mind that I am a lawyer, and I think I have heard a lot of nonsensical excuses in my line of work. She told me that she was trying to prepare dinner for the following day. Her answer was pitiful, and she realized it immediately too. She knew she had been caught with her hand in the cookie jar. The really sad part was that whenever she felt she may not easily get out of it, then she will make the experience so terrible in order to make me lose interest in asking her next time. Being with her became like hospital food when you are on admission. Though it can be wonderful, fantastic, and taste incredibly great, most times you have to be starving almost to death to make yourself consume it. Desiree will also deliberately pick a fight over trifles. She reasons that if we are not in good times or if we are fighting, I will not be asking for her treasures down below."

"How so?" Adam asked.

"For instance, one Saturday morning, I wanted to work at home on an office project that I could not finish on Friday. Unfortunately, I forgot some of the needed documents at work and I had to go to the office to pick them up. She called me on the way and asked me to buy bread on my way back, but she did not specify what type of bread. I stopped by the grocery store close to my work in the District of Columbia and I bought two loaves of wheat bread. When I delivered them to her in the kitchen, she shouted at me that I bought the wrong bread."

"What do you mean by wrong bread?" I asked. I thought we always eat wheat bread.

"No, this is not the right wheat bread. You bought whole wheat bread. You were supposed to buy honey wheat bread," she yelled.

"What is the big deal about that?" I remarked. I then tried to diffuse the tension and said, "If the issue is the honey, we have honey at home. Just sprinkle some on the wheat bread and we have our own fresh homemade honey wheat bread."

"Desiree did not find this funny at all. She kept on talking and talking, on and on for a very long time. She took a cup and put it down without doing anything with it. Then, she took a pot from the cabinet and placed it on the granite counter top without doing anything with it. She just kept complaining. She later took a plate and placed it on the cooking pot and placed the pot cover on the plate and cooking pot with both being empty. At this point, I felt something was grossly wrong. So, I asked her if everything was okay with her. She retorted that she did not tell me that anything was wrong with her. As I turned to leave her in peace since I wasn't making any headway, she told me to go and return the bread. It sounded like a bad joke."

"Let me get this straight. You want me to drive fifteen miles to DC and fifteen miles back home in order to return two loaves of bread," I sought clarification.

"Yes," she replied.

"And that makes sense to you?" I asked with a tiny bit of sarcasm.

"Yes," she affirmed.

"No. You must be joking," I turned away and left. After some minutes, I returned to the kitchen, I tore one of the loaves of bread, took out a slice and ate it. Then, I turned to her and said, "You see, there is nothing wrong with this bread. We can manage it. I will remember honey wheat bread next time." From my perspective, this was not only to make her realize that the wheat bread was okay, but also to show her in a nice and relatively non-confrontational way that I was not going to return the bread. However, Desiree did not take this lightly. She just kept quiet. At night when we retired to bed, I wanted us to go to wonderland in between the sheets. She started yelling and complaining about the stupid wheat bread from the morning. It was unbelievable. I tried as much as I could to calm down because I already knew that this was just a ploy for her to get away from her comfort duty to me.

So, I held her right hand and said to her, "My dear, if we are having a disagreement or even in a worst-case scenario, if we are fighting, that does not mean we cannot travel to the land of pleasure together."

"Leave me alone," she replied. "We cannot be doing anything together if we are fighting. This is about my how I feel."

"Okay, let us resolve our differences," I said trying to reach a very necessary quick settlement.

"Return the wheat bread," she blurted.

"The partially eaten wheat bread from this morning?" I asked, being quite surprised.

"The other loaf has not been opened," she noted.

"You are unbelievable," I replied, being unable to hide my frustration. She just said no throughout. I fell asleep that night with profound anger. I didn't talk to her for two days afterwards. Then, it dawned on me that she had her way. She achieved what she set out to accomplish which was to ensure that there will be no action for my passion. She accomplished her objective. She won. I lost.

Out of the blue, Adam chuckled. His friends looked at him wondering what was going on in his befogged mind.

"I just remembered a question that I was asked by Dr. Omar Omonla many years ago," Adam explained.

"The same Dr. Omar Omonla of the Doctor from Mamuria fame?" Ray asked.

"Yes, the one and only," Adam replied.

"You knew him personally?" Ray asked being surprised.

"Of course. We were buddies during our residency training in Internal Medicine together. He later went to specialize in infectious diseases."

"So, what happened?" Kamal inquired.

"When Omar first came to the United States, he was fascinated by the Star-Spangled Banner and how often we pay homage to the flag at many functions and sporting events. He read the anthem and compared it with Mamuria's National anthem. He later asked me what we meant by the land of the free and the home of the brave. I teased him saying that the land of the free means that the women are free. They do whatever they want and get away with it. That was why the statue of liberty is female. Then I informed him that the brave are the men who put up with them. So, listening to how badly Desiree is treating you is really making me think that maybe I was correct. It really takes a brave man to put up with a woman who thinks she is free to do whatever she wants and refuses her husband as she pleases. Congratulations, Ray. You are officially a brave man," Adam concluded with sarcasm.

Ray turned to Kamal and remarked, "This is wrong. It is unfair."

Kamal agreed and asked, "But what can we do?"

"It is a bad move for any woman to deny her husband's request on the basis of a fight. I mean, if they are fighting and he still wants her, it is because they can easily resolve their differences. It is going to help solve the problem. However, if it doesn't, they can resume their fight afterwards. That will only make it a true sweet and sour tango. It will be like a timed ceasefire during a battle. You can spend the time to bury the dead, attend to the wounded, get comfort packages to those trapped in war and get reinforcement for the soldiers. It does not mean that the war is over. I think it is just humane," Ray opined.

"I know that women will often say that it is their mental state issues, but what about the man's mental state issue too?" Adam queried.

Healing with the Dealing
When he approaches you for that dealing
To help him take care of that feeling
Please don't say no to his calling
Just because you're quarrelling
Doing it may not be appealing
But coming to his arms rather than leaving
Will put you on the path of marital healing

"After sometime, I guess that she got 'empowered,' using the new marriage-ruining buzzword from single mothers everywhere. It was as if she was trying to sign up for membership in SMN."

"What is SMN?" Adam inquired.

"Single Mothers' Network," Ray replied. It is my way of describing those single people who give marriage ruining advice to unsuspecting wives. Anyway, Desiree has stopped pretending to be sick. She is no longer making excuses for saying no. She will just tell me straight up to leave her alone," Ray continued.

"She constantly told me that it is her body and she has the right to say no as she pleases. I started wondering if she was getting her fix somewhere else. It got so bad that I started thinking of what to do including divorcing her. Eventually, I had to open up to my sister who had come to visit us when she realized that there were major problems in my kingdom. She recommended finding a female family counselor. So, I brought up the idea of seeking professional help for our marriage and Desiree agreed. I actually allowed her to pick any counselor she wanted, and she picked one Dr. Nitah Witherspoon. I call her Dr. Nit Wit. She was ridiculous to say the least. We went to her office in an upscale part of the Metro area in Bethesda. You would think that by being in the same city as the National Institute of Health that she will have some useful knowledge by passive diffusion from breathing air close to the mother of all research institutions.

After we had explained what was going on to her and I complained that I wasn't getting enough attention, she had the nerve to quiz me. She asked me many ridiculous questions like, *How many times have you written poems for her like you used to do before marriage? How many times have you given her a day off at home so that you let her be a woman and treat herself to feminine things? How often do you take her out to dinner just the two of you to give her some respite from the battalion of children you squeezed out of her in close succession?* She went on and on pestering me with these insane questions. It was as if I was on trial for neglect or abuse or something. In the end, she suggested that I should go and join a gym to burn some calories every night so that I don't have too much energy for an exhausted housewife. I could not believe it. I actually thought maybe she was a fake doctor and I later checked her credentials. To my surprise, she was really a genuine allopathic doctor. I still think the medical board should seize her certificate and suspend her practice license.

I voiced my opinion that I feel that this issue of "No means No" is applicable for boyfriends and girlfriends who are not married. I also mentioned to them that a husband should not be told that he is lucky when his wife says yes to be in between the sheets with him. After all, husbands don't tell their wives and children that they are lucky when they do their responsibilities. A lot of time, the husband has to suck it up and do a job he does not like. He swallows his pride and put up with a boss that he detests so that he can pay the house rent, put food on the table, pay the school fees of the children and buy clothes for them. It was a really contentious consultation. Later, I noticed that Dr. Nit Wit doesn't have a wedding ring even though she looks quite mature.

"We argued back and forth for a while, with both Desiree and Dr. Nit Wit conspiring against mankind. After trying quite unsuccessfully for them to be reasonable, I decided to change strategy and I went on a defensive offense. I turned to Dr. Nit Wit and addressed her directly."

"So, if my wife is feeling tired of cooking, can I order take out or get somebody to assist her with the cooking in the house?" I asked her.

"Of course, yes," came a very quick response and her face came to life with a smile.

"And you think that if she is tired of cleaning her own home, I could contract a cleaning services company to help out without hurting her feelings?" I continued.

"Absolutely," she replied. "I don't think she will mind that at all."

"So, if she does not feel like comforting me between the sheets, I can get somebody else to lend her a hand in that regard also?" I asked while trying to look genuine in my inquisition.

"No, you can't," came the reply simultaneously from her and my wife who had hitherto been quiet and just nodding to the mountain of support she had been getting from Dr. Nit Wit.

"Why not?" I asked rhetorically. "It is still trying to help her in her duties," I noted.

"Afterwards, my wife and Dr. Nit Wit just kept saying things that I cannot vividly recall, but they made absolutely no sense at all," Ray concluded.

He then turned to his friends and opined, "I think that a wife who is constantly refusing to share her husband's bed for whatever bogus reason is in dereliction of duty."

"I agree," Adam and Kamal replied in unison.

(**Author's note: Poll for readers:** If a wife frequently and persistently denies her husband of intimacy, is he justified to have extramarital affairs? Please go to blissfulgardenz.com.)

"How many times should a wife be excused for saying no to her husband before he is allowed to seek an alternate source of comfort?" Adam asked.

"Think baseball. Three strikes," Ray suggested, quickly noting that the issue under consideration is a game of balls and sticks too.

Adam and Kamal nodded their heads in agreement. The suggestion was reasonable to them.

"If a wife says no to her husband's love advances without serious justifications three times, he should feel free to go and take care of himself," Ray continued his ranting. "We need to address this issue as a society. It is ridiculous how men get treated in this regard. You may have a man who is not getting enough or may not even be getting anything at home with all these nonsensical, *leave me alone, it is my body, I am not interested* excuses raining constantly on him from his wife, and nobody condemns that. The poor guy gets treated as if he is married to a nun and he gets *none*. Now, when the man seeks his succor somewhere else, then society accuses him of cheating on his wife and being unfaithful to some stupid vows, and expects him to apologize. I really think that the wife should be the one to apologize for putting her husband in that predicament. She should be the one who stands behind those microphones in the press conference to say *I failed in my sacred duty. I did not keep my vow to honor my husband. I failed my husband. Please forgive me.* Enough of all this rubbish! If a man is accused of having extramarital affairs, we should first ask him if he is getting enough from his wife," Ray opined.

"I totally agree with you. Going into a marriage is like a trade between a buyer and a seller," Adam chimed in facing Ray.

"Who is the buyer and who is the seller?" Kamal inquired.

"Of course, the woman is the seller and the man is the buyer. This is always a sellers' market. That is why the man is seeking the woman to accept his proposal and negotiate things like marriage gifts, dowry in some cultures, those dinners and movies, et cetera," Adam replied.

"So, if marriage is a trade, what are they trading?" Kamal asked sarcastically.

"Body fluids!" Adam replied with a straight face. He then turned directly to make an eye contact with Kamal and said, "I agree with Ray. In my candid opinion, if a wife keeps telling her husband to leave her alone, she is saying to him in a very clear language to take his business elsewhere. It is akin to daring him to find the same product elsewhere."

"Anyway, let me conclude what happened in Dr. Nit Wit's

office," Ray continued. "At the end of the consultation, she suggested to my wife to try and accommodate me once or twice a week. They both made it sound as if they were doing me a favor. I felt as if I was in an extra special marital solitary confinement where they will allow my manhood to leave its prison once or twice a week. I still could not wrap my head around the belief that a wife can tell her husband that he is lucky when she allows him to get between her legs. Shouldn't it be obvious to everybody that he is entitled to it? Why else did he marry her?" Ray asked rhetorically.

"I was still very upset when we left the doctor's office, but I was determined to make it work. Twice a week is surely better than twice a month, I submitted, even though it was still grossly insufficient. Unfortunately, things did not get better. Rather, my wife adopted BAM."

"What is BAM?" Adam asked

"It is a term I coined for the sort of intimacy she was giving me afterwards. It is Banging a Mannequin."

"Have you banged a mannequin before?" Kamal inquired midway between been serious and joking.

"Of course not," Ray replied, "but I can't imagine it being worse. I think banging a real mannequin may even be better. At least the mannequin is not going to be cursing you. I mean, Desiree will just lie down there like a piece of wood. Her demeanor will be akin to *just do whatever you want and leave me alone.* It was horrible. Should a wife cook badly because her husband likes her food, but he is gaining weight and she wants him to lose weight? Should a wife be terrible in bed to discourage her husband from bothering her?" Ray asked rhetorically.

She is Breaking My Heart
When I am in the mood
She lies down like a piece of wood
Instead of acting like a queen
She stays motionless like a mannequin

"I couldn't help being cranky all the time. I lost interest in playing with our children. I see all of them as extensions of their mother who is constantly maltreating me. A few months later, I got to the point of thinking of divorcing her to salvage whatever was left of my dignity and manhood. Unfortunately, we got a distress call from Patricia's teacher from school asking us to come for a parent-teacher conference together. I thought it was odd, but I wanted to know what was going on. So, we went to meet her teacher. She showed us what Patricia had written as her class assignment on animals."

Animals

If I have wings like a bird of prey
I will surely fly away
From mummy and daddy

If I can run fast like a cheetah
I will surely run away
From mummy and daddy

If I can swim like a shark
I will sure swim away
From mummy and daddy

"Honestly, I was heartbroken. Her poetry sounded great, but the message was a disaster. She was feeling all the tension at home and I had not noticed it. I actually thought the children were too young to notice that anything was amiss. I also felt that they were all on the side of their mother from whatever she intoxicated them with from her breast milk. It seemed that the kids were bearing the brunt of this impasse. So, I decided to give Dr. Nit Wit's suggestions a trial, maybe we can press a pause button or a reset button and get our acts together. I paid Brenda, our neighbor's daughter, to watch the kids while I took Desiree to a luxurious restaurant for dinner a few days later. I gave Brenda our cell phone numbers, the restaurant's phone number, and a key to our reserve car with instruction to call us for anything of concern. I gave Desiree a dozen roses, a box of her favorite chocolate and a card in which I had written a fence-mending poem."

Holding on

Being with you
Brings me comfort and happiness

Eating with you
Brings me strength and joyfulness
Talking with you
Brings me joy and I avoid loneliness
Sharing with you
Brings me health and cheerfulness
Going with you
Brings me life and lightheartedness
Intimacy with you
Brings me satisfaction and blissfulness
Arguing with you
Brings me sorrow and gloominess
Fighting with you
Brings me misery and profound sadness
Let's hang on to hope
After all we are not on dope
Let's hang in there.
Let's not give up here.
I love you

"She read the card and seemed to be very happy. I was elated thinking we are getting back on track. I thought that it was going to be like the good old days and she would come flying back home to Papa. How wrong I was! The dinner date was a disaster. She was constantly calling home every five minutes to ask about the children. It was annoying! She called Brenda to ask if the children were playing. She called back to ask if they were thirsty. She called to ask if they were not fighting. She called to ask if any of the children used the restroom. Believe me, by the time she called Brenda wanting to talk to each child, I realized that she did not want to be with me at all. It was too obvious that she would rather be with her children. The dinner date was a colossal waste of time and money and I lost my appetite. I was just an unfortunate bystander in her life. I felt used. It was as if she just wanted me around to fertilize her eggs whenever she wanted and spend money on her children. Well, maybe I should be thankful that we are not a species of Praying Mantis, that the females eat the males after reproduction. Who knows, maybe this is even her own version of cannibalizing her male partner," Ray concluded with dejection.

"Maybe you should think of something positive about her? That may help you get through these tough times," Kamal suggested.

"There is nothing positive about a wife who keeps her husband hungry and thirsty in the midst of plenty," Ray replied and renewed his ranting. "I wonder whatever is going on in the minds of these so-called human and animal rights bigots. If a person ties down her cat or dog and did not feed it, all the animal rights people will carry placards. Yet, our society not only condones, but overtly encourages a woman to tie her husband down and not comfort him. This is certainly an emotional abuse that women deliberately inflict on good husbands. This is a human rights abuse that nobody is addressing. If a woman allows somebody who is not married to her to get in between her legs, I guess he is lucky, and he will probably feel lucky too. This will never be applicable to her husband. It is his right, and he is entitled to it. This ridiculous mentality of women thinking that they can have their cakes and eat them too needs serious reevaluation. This may be part of the reasons why marriages are not lasting long, and men are choosing not to marry. After all, if we put morality aside, for quite successful men it is cheaper not to marry and you can have as many girlfriends with full benefits as you want. Why be responsible for a woman and her children if you can get away with just paying child support? Moreover, if you don't even want children, a quick trip to your urologist for vasectomy will prevent child support from chasing you anywhere. Furthermore, it is not too difficult that dinner alone even without the movie can get you savoring the forbidden fruit. Wise women would not say no to their husbands."

Ray took a sip of his drink and continued his ranting, "Another thing that makes me really crazy is that Desiree does not attend to my needs anymore, even outside the sheets. For instance, when I come home from work, she is quick to point out that there is left over rice in the fridge that I should microwave it if I want to eat. There is nothing like serving me my food. Meanwhile, she will always attend to the flimsy requests from her children. Whenever, I complain and raise this issue with her, she is always reminding me that these are my children. She is quick to point out that I am a grown man and should be able to take care of myself. So, imagine my horror when we were at a social function and somebody asked her about her children and she responded that she has four children and I am her fifth child. I was livid and rebuked her never to ever say such a thing ever again, that it was an insult. Although I later felt bad for rebuking her in public, but I had a lot of pent-up anger."

Ray later continued after a pause. "A few weeks after this disastrous outing, I remembered a popular saying that friends do influence friends, and I really thought that I had found a possible angle that could help resolve our issue."

Part One: Section Three:
Before the Ocean Dries Up

I really could not help thinking that if a wife is not answering the call of her husband or she is frequently struggling with answering the call of her husband adequately, the husband should have the right to call another girl to help his wife. So, I thought of calling her friends for help," Ray continued.

At this point Adam gave a sigh of relief and smiled. This made Ray pause.

"Who did you think I was going to call?" he asked Adam with a lot of curiosity.

"Em... em... ghostbusters?" Adam replied and burst into an uncontrollable laughter.

"You were thinking, that I was going to call a call girl, weren't you?" Ray asked.

"I invoke the fifth amendment on that one," Adam replied. "But think about it for a minute, you used the word *call* three times in a sentence while talking about a girl."

Ray shook his head and continued. "When I analyzed her friends, that was when it hit me that her friends may actually be contributing significantly to the problem," Ray concluded.

"What made you think so?" Kamal asked.

Ray continued. "Desiree has three main friends and they have been close for quite some time. They are Susan, Renee and

Mercedes. Susan is a high end, high maintenance career lady. She lives in The Excelsior, a luxury apartment in Georgetown in the District of Columbia. She is very flamboyant in public but extremely lonely in private. The few times that I have heard her speak to my wife she was always lamenting that she missed her chance to marry a nice young immigrant from Ghana a few years ago when she was still looking for the perfect knight on a white horse. Now, it seems that people tend to think that she is way out of their league and nobody is knocking on her door anymore. She claims that men have developed a serious inferiority complex around her."

"Renee has never been married to the best of my knowledge, but men change more frequently in her life than oil changes in Jiffy Lube. She now has three children from three fathers and they are currently in paternity dispute over the last child, who is only nine months old."

"Mercedes is in a class of her own. She is really Mercedes H class."

"H class? I do not recall that there is such a class," Adam inquired looking puzzled.

"Mercedes H class is Mercedes Horrible class."

"I see," Adam submitted.

Ray continued. "I actually know her husband very well, because I have been asked previously to speak to him regarding his family and act as a mediator in their marital discord."

"Sounds disturbingly interesting, what happened?" Adam asked out of curiosity.

"Diamond Cooper is her ex-husband. The first piece of advice he gave me when I met him was: 'Do not marry any girl who is named after a car because she will drive you crazy.'"

"Mercedes is a beautiful woman with a sharp tongue and an ungrateful heart that is never satisfied." Diamond had said. "If I cut my head for her, she will still complain that I left some neck behind," he claimed.

"His story was that Mercedes was never satisfied. She belittled everything her husband had done for her because she always wanted what others had. She always thought that her husband did not measure up. She works as an Administrative Secretary for a plumbing company. However, she believes that she must drive a Mercedes Benz as the only car that befits her.

She doesn't assist with any bills and spends all her money paying a car note on her Mercedes Benz Sports Utility Vehicle. The husband told me that whenever they have a misunderstanding, rather than calling him by his name Diamond Cooper, Mercedes will make a mockery of his name by calling him 'Copper mini Cooper.' Diamond related an incident to me to buttress his point about how terrible Mercedes had been to him. He related that Mercedes was constantly complaining that their family was the only one still living in an apartment complex when everybody else lived in single family houses with multiple car garages."

"After so much bickering, he decided to move, and they bought a town house that he could barely afford to pay the mortgage on despite working two jobs at that time. A few weeks later, it was their wedding anniversary and she wanted them to celebrate it. However, she booked an extremely high-end restaurant called Heavenly Taste on K Street in Washington DC. He had no idea how expensive this restaurant was, but he thought their motto was bold and intriguing."

"What was the motto?" Kamal inquired.

"A taste of heaven on earth," Ray replied.

"Nice!" Kamal responded.

"Anyway," Ray continued. "Diamond said that the restaurant served ordinary dishes but called them with incredible adjectives just to charge an arm and a leg for them."

Kamal chuckled and asked, "Like what?"

"I don't vividly remember all of them, but he mentioned things like *Fantastic Fries, Superb Soup, Salutary Salmon, Delightful Deli*, et cetera. The serving portion size was very small and incredibly expensive.

"I guess they were charging for the adjectives they used to qualify the menu," Kamal remarked while laughing.

"Four medium sized shrimp with tartar sauce dipping was $25 on the menu. A glass of soda was $10. In the end they had a pediatric dose menu of salmon, mashed potato, spinach and a slice of cheesecake dessert each. By the time the tax and 15% gratuity were added to their bill, it came to $285. The worse part of it was that he was still hungry. When he saw the bill, his eyes almost popped out of their sockets. At this point, Mercedes cracked a callous joke saying, 'It does not matter whether you use your right or your left, so long as you just foot the bill,' and laughed. It was the most insensitive joke ever according to Diamond. His divorce from

Mercedes was concluded about six months ago," Ray concluded.

"When I realized that Desiree's friends are bad influences, I knew that engaging them would be a waste of time. I started contemplating divorce, but I kept talking myself out of it for the sake of our children."

"However, on Saturday morning about three months ago, she had another round of her insulting moments of *Leave me alone, Can't you keep your pants on? Is this all you think about every day? It is not food. Can't you think of something better to do?* and *Stop bothering me*. At that point, I had had enough of putting up with this nonsense. This is an unfair world against honest, faithful, loyal, committed, hardworking, and family-focused men. It is unfair. If the shoe was on the other foot, everybody will call for my head. Think about it this way, if she works hard for the money, she will demand that she be treated right. Why is it then that I am doing my responsibilities as the man of the house, as a husband and father, but I do not get to be treated right? I should be treated right. We have to be fair. We simply have to apply the balanced principle that what is good for the goose is good for the gander. The society will condemn me, and the court system will come after me for child and spousal support if I was failing in my duties. However, my wife is failing in her duties to me and nobody cares. It is very obvious that when a wife turns her husband down and leaves him in the cold, it is a humongous emotional abuse. I think The United States Congress needs to come together quickly and enact a law to protect men from this nonsensical marital emotional abuse constantly committed against husbands. The President of the United States should also sign it into law immediately."

"What I even find more annoying is that women then act so surprised that their husbands become very angry after they rip their hearts out with their stupid, incessant and callous *No, leave me alone!* rejections. I am sure that it does not take rocket science to figure out that when a man approaches his wife, he is picturing both of them on lofty love heights and on their way to touch the sky. All of a sudden, she pushes him away with her callous *No* from the top of a sky scrapper and the poor guy lands on his head. Then, the wife wants to act innocently and wonder why he is so angry. It is ridiculous."

"I agree with you. Women need to appreciate this. The fastest way to ruin their marriages is to keep saying *No* to their husbands," Adam opined.

Ray continued, "I decided to move on. After about one hour of working on my computer while sitting on the couch in the living room, I felt Desiree's hand on my shoulder and she said, "I am sorry." I was surprised. I had been so angry and so engrossed in what I was doing that I did not realize that she had been looking over my shoulders at my computer screen. She realized that I was in the process of renting a relatively inexpensive one-bedroom apartment in Capital Heights at the border of the District of Columbia. I guess that made her realize that she had gone too far. I told her to leave me alone. Later that afternoon, I got a call from Mama Wise that she wanted to see me and my wife. Ms. Hikmah is everybody's mother in our community. We all call her Mama Wise because of her wisdom and experience in counseling couples going through challenges. She is not a formally trained psychologist or counselor as far as I know, but she is well respected for her honesty, generosity and fairness in the community according to the grapevine information I had about her. Apparently, Desiree somehow realized that she was about to crash her marriage to me and somebody had advised her to seek help from Mama Wise. When we went to see Mama Wise that evening, I did not know what to expect. The last time I had talked to another woman about this issue, it was Dr. Nit Wit and she formed an estrogen alliance with my wife against me. Mama Wise may be different, but I was convinced that women are all the same. It is the XX chromosome thing. Of course, XX means you are wrong twice. For a man, it is XY chromosome, meaning that you are wrong only once out every two attempts. That was my thinking," Ray revealed.

"You and your pseudo-science! Anyway, what happened?" Adam inquired.

"Mama Wise lives in a simple two-bedroom apartment, nothing fancy. I knew she was a widow and lived alone. Her husband had died two years previously and her children are all grown up and live in different parts of the country. My wife and I related to her what was going on, and I told her bluntly that I was fed up. To my utmost surprise, Mama Wise actually blamed Desiree without mincing words. She told her to get her priorities right. I was shocked when she told her that her husband is her closest family member and should be treated as number one. In fact, she went as far as reminding her in a very soft and concerning manner that Desiree should realize that children should not upstage their father."

"My daughter," she said to Desiree, "build a great relationship with your husband because after a short time, your children will grow up and they will leave the house. That is when it will strike you that they are not your world, but your transient responsibility. You will be left with your husband. If you did not have a great relationship with him now, it will be too late to build any relationship then. Remember that your children may show you that they love you, but they will still prefer that you do not come and live with them. The fact is that they will also want to build their own future with their own families. My daughter, do not frustrate your husband into thinking that there has got to be another woman out there who may not look as beautiful as you, as gorgeous as you, but will still be good enough to meet his needs," she advised Desiree. "My deceased husband, Mr. Longfellow, was not my first husband. He was my second husband. I was first widowed when I was thirty-nine years old and I had five children in my first marriage. It is a long story my dear. Maybe another day, I may tell you my story. Right now, I want you to take good care of your husband for me. I hope you will do that for me," she concluded while patting Desiree to console her, as she was crying at this point.

"Honestly, I was stunned," Ray continued. "I have always believed that women never tell one another the truth. I assumed wrongly that women are too sensitive of their feelings that they do not want to hurt anybody emotionally. Therefore, they will just wallow in self-deceit. Boy, I was happy to be wrong. It is ironic, isn't it?" Ray asked.

Adam and Kamal were short of words, but nodded in agreement.

"So, how are things between you and Desiree now?" Kamal asked Ray after a pause.

"Things got a lot better after the intervention by Mama Wise, but it only lasted for about a month; gradually, Desiree went back to her old ways to a great extent. I am still not happy, and I am still very lonely. Interestingly, two weeks ago I was wondering how many husbands in the United States are suffering and pretending to be smiling like me. I went on the web and I was surprised to find a support group for men. I couldn't believe it. Have you ever heard of a shelter for men who have experienced domestic abuse or a center for battered men before?" he asked his friends.

"No," Adam and Kamal replied.

"Exactly my point. However, I was intrigued when I found a support group on the internet called "Organization for Oppressed Husbands (OOH)," Ray explained.

"OOH sounds like moaning when somebody hit you in the crotch. Well, I guess whoever is a member of this group must have been kicked in the you-know-where by his wife," Kamal concluded.

"I realized that this group is actually fairly local, and they meet in Annapolis, just a few blocks from the State House," Ray continued. "I was curious. I emailed their coordinator who also happened to be the founder of the organization. His name is Mr. Buster Ball. I was amused about his name in terms of *Bust* and *Ball*. Anyway, he replied and invited me to come over to their next meeting. Last Saturday, thirteen men including myself met at his house in his basement. I am sure that I don't need to tell you that he lives alone now. Some of the men are still married while others are at various stages in the separation and divorce continuum."

"After a brief introduction, people readily shared their stories and updated the group on what was going on, status updates of some sort, you may say. They were all unpleasant tales. After listening to them, you will conclude that women are the number one source of woes to men. Later, I realized that they were deliberately pronouncing women as 'woe-men' not 'wi-men.' Then Buster requested Dave to share his story with me. Dave seemed to be a gentleman with blunted affect. His story was that he dropped out of a four-year college after completing the first year. This was because Emily, his childhood sweetheart who was just finishing high school, was going through a difficult time due to a bitter ongoing divorce of her parents and had nowhere to stay. Her grandmother had taken her in only for her to die suddenly of a massive heart attack two months later. So, Dave dropped out of college to help Emily, contrary to the advice of his parents. He initially worked simple jobs to be able to afford a studio apartment and support the two of them. Although they struggled to make ends meet, he encouraged her to go to school while he worked since he was very good with his hands. He eventually obtained a vocational degree in heating, ventilation and air conditioning (HVAC) systems. Eventually, they got married after a few years of living together. They have a son who they named Gabriel. Dave explained that they chose Gabriel because the angel brought a lot of good news and they were in dire need at that time. No doubt, Emily is very intelligent and was an honor student. So, she continued her studies while Dave worked to support the family. Eventually, Emily obtained a Bachelor and Master's degree in Systems and Computer Science. She later obtained a Master of Business Administration (MBA) degree to increase her profile for a top tier job. Now, she is a senior manager in the Information Technology department of a major utility company in the Washington Metropolitan area."

"The unfortunate development was that Emily kept looking down on Dave because she makes a lot more money. According to Dave, his wife is now 'swimming with the sharks in the big league.' Every time they have a small misunderstanding, she is always quick to point out to him that she is the one who wears the pant in their family and that without her they would not be living in a four-bedroom house with two car garages in a very good neighborhood. Dave related that what pains him the most is whenever Emily tells him that she has two Master's degrees unlike Dave who has a 'half degree.' 'I think they should call what you have a *deg* and remove the *ree* from it to accurately reflect what it really is,' Emily would constantly say."

"I could not believe how bad Dave's situation was, and I sympathized with him," Ray opined shaking his head and pitying the ordeal being faced by Dave.

"No, that is not the end of the story. Buster chimed in. He is just getting to the good part."

"Lay it on me, brother. I really want to know what happened," Ray recalled telling Dave.

Leggo Your Ego

The fact that you now have more money
Does not stop me from being your honey
I know you read the book
But you surely know what it took

I know you did all the reading
But don't reduce me to always pleading
I have always given you your right
Don't let your success blind your sight

Dave continued his story with all oppressed husbands listening on. "So, a few months ago at our meeting here, it was suggested that I fight back, and we discussed what I should do next time she insults me like that. Surely the day came about a week later and I was ready for her. I let her finish telling me how much she has accomplished and how I am a lowly person compared to her. Then I brought out a thermometer as we have discussed here. I showed her a thermometer and said to her, 'Emily, it is true that you have more degrees than me. However, this thermometer has more degrees than you. I am sure that Ms. Educated with two Master's degrees knows that the best thermometers are the useful ones and the useful ones are the accurate ones and the accurate ones are the ones that measure core body temperatures. Guess where they go, Ms. educated? I asked rhetorically. They go into the anus as rectal thermometers in spite of all their degrees. So take your stupid degrees and shove them into where the sun does not shine. You ungrateful arrogant woman!' Dave shouted wagging his pointed index finger in demonstration of how it all went down."

"All of us jubilated with Dave. We were pumping our fists and clapping in celebration with Dave. I must say, it felt really good," Ray recalled.

Adam and Kamal were laughing hysterically too.

"Oh my God! That was a perfect response," Kamal opined.

"What did she say?" Adam asked.

"Dave said that Emily was shocked at the response and she walked away. However, two days later she was a real daughter of the Hell's Queen, and Dave decided to leave the house. The fantastic part of the story is that Dave now lives happily by himself in a studio apartment in Washington DC and has enrolled to study Electrical Engineering in Potomac University in Washington DC in the fall. It was an interesting experience listening to those guys. I will probably attend the meeting next month," Ray concluded.

Love should be refreshing like the breeze of the bay at Annapolis.

"Ray, I am still of the opinion that you should try and work things out with Desiree. I am somewhat still optimistic that things will work out in the end. It is hard for me to think that you guys should head for the rocks. I mean, you have four children who will be better off with mummy and daddy," Adam stated.

"Maybe Ray is the one that is not taking her to the mountain top and that is why she lost interest," Kamal suggested with tongue in cheek.

"No way," Ray replied while flexing his muscles and contracting his biceps.

"Bro, that is not the right muscle for the job," Kamal noted and they all laughed.

"Seriously, discuss with her," Kamal suggested. "I know that sometimes, a man may think that when he is satisfied, the woman is satisfied too. However, this may not be the case. Moreover, some ladies are too shy to bring the issue up with their husbands, so they embark on 'civil disobedience' rather than expressing the root cause of the problem. I think you should ask her why she lost interest. You should get in shape too. Be strong to do stack three rounds," Kamal recommended.

"Why three rounds?" Ray inquired looking puzzled.

"It is believed that the first round is for you, the second round is for her and the third round gets you all the privileges in the world. That is when she will call you daddy," Kamal explained.

"Interesting! I hear you, but I don't think that it has anything to do with me," Ray countered.

"Would you say that you've gained some weight since you got married?" Kamal asked.

"Yes, a little bit. I weighed one hundred and seventy pounds before we got married," Ray replied.

"And now?" Kamal asked.

"About two hundred and fifteen pounds," Ray answered.

"That means that you've gained, you know, forty-five pounds. Maybe she doesn't see you the way she used to," Kamal opined.

"My weight gain is her fault too. She is a great cook, but doesn't let me burn the calories by doing the exercise that I need with her," Ray replied while laughing.

"Maybe it will help if you lose some weight, shower your wife with affection and gifts, and help in the house a bit—do the dishes, laundry, cook or order food sometimes—to give her a break. You should also consider giving her occasional days off too. You could take the kids away for a whole day during which you can bond with your children and your wife will also have some me-time too," Kamal suggested.

"Do a passby before you need a bypass," Adam chimed in.

"I understand bypass. That is when the surgeons reduce the size of the stomach to make obese people lose weight, what is a passby?"

"It is really simple. It is when you see food and you simply "pass by" it," Adam explained laughing.

"I hear you, but let us face it. Do wives really have the right to deny their husbands? I mean, in a monogamous relationship, the man has to actively suppress his instinct to stay with his wife rather than going on a prowl. A man in a monogamous relationship is a beast who is locked up in a cardboard cage. He knows that he can always get out anytime he wants, but he chooses to stay in the cage. If the handler, his wife in this case, decides to constantly maltreat him by denying him his needs, he is simply going to walk out of the cardboard cage and it will be impossible to keep him there ever again," Ray offered his opinion.

"I really think that women need to know the instinct of men. A man may be standing next to his wife who happens to be the most beautiful woman in the world. Yet, if another woman who is fifty percent less attractive passes in front of him, his animal instinct is still to look at her even though his wife is the most beautiful woman in the world and she is standing right there with him. What then do women think will be happening in a man's mind if the wife is now rejecting him constantly, making him hungry and thirsty for the forbidden fruit?," Ray asked.

Then, there was a moment of putrid silence.

"Hey, I have an idea," Kamal uttered looking excited and pointing to Ray. "Why not pretend as if you are doing a PSA to all women in the world on this issue?"

"PSA for women? Did you mean Prostate Specific Antigen?" Adam inquired looking puzzled.

"No, Doc. Don't think about medicine all the time. PSA is Public Service Announcement," Kamal explained.

Ray cleared his throat and pretended to be holding a microphone. With a genuine concerned voice, he said:

The Public Service Announcement from Ray Marshall
"Dear females of the seven continents

The babes of Africa
The hotties of Antarctica
The chicks of Asia
The beauties of Australia
The dames of Europe
The ladies of North America
The bombshells of South America

Daughters of every land
Wives of every country
Mothers of every continent

Please indulge me in my passionate appeal.
Contrary to what it may appear to be
Different from what the situation may seem to be
All men truly want to have peace
And most men are very easy to please

Let him feel your love and respect him

Don't deny your husband anything
That you want to be the only one giving him
Never give him any reasons to think
That there has to be another woman out there
Who could be better than you

Don't let your children upstage your husband
You will be left with him when the children are gone
Don't hold your responsibility as a hostage
While you are trying to demand your right
It is better to do your responsibility
And then claim your right
I wish you well.

Please talk to my wife to stop maltreating me."

Kamal responded, "But they don't know your wife."
"True. But if every woman everywhere discusses these with her friends, it will eventually get to her," Ray concluded.

Part Two

Garlands for the Patient:
The Story of Kamal

Part Two: Section One:
Late to the Party

So how are things with you, Kamal?" Ray asked.
"I wish I could say that I'm fine," he replied.
"Why?" Adam chipped in.
"Because I am caught between an emotional rock and a responsibility hard place," Kamal replied. "I am struggling with balancing my life between my current wife, Bonita and my ex-wife, Kandie. Bonita is my true soulmate but we don't have any children together yet. Unfortunately, Kandie happens to be the mother of my only child, Kamal Junior. It has been really tough."

Then, Kamal proceeded and related to his friends how he ended up in his current predicament. After he left high school, he enrolled in Annapolis Community College in Annapolis, Maryland. The goal was for him to eventually study Business Administration. Unfortunately, youthful exuberance got the best of him. He was so eager to get away from home. He wanted it all. He lived in an apartment that he shared with Troy, another student. Troy had just transferred from a four-year college to a community college. In retrospect, that was a text book definition of an unusual retrogression. Troy was eager to explore the world too. He and Kamal felt truly free. They had found liberty away from home. It was freedom at last! They were away from home, away from parents, away from being bothered, and away from being told constantly what to do.

Troy, his roommate, was a lot of fun. Nothing bothered him. He seemed to have everything all figured out. There were many school days that he did not leave the apartment at all. Kamal mused, and then he chuckled about something he remembered. There were many days that he did not go to school too. Thinking back, he just could not figure out what they actually did with all the time they spent away from school.

At the end of his first academic year, his grade point average was 2.0. His father was very angry. The goal he had set for himself was to do better in the next academic year; unfortunately, his foundation knowledge was too weak. He struggled a lot in the first semester of his second year. He had to meet his academic counselor too many times that even the counselor started sounding like his father. Although his GPA improved to 2.3, he did not think he was doing great. He felt he needed a break. Somehow, he started thinking about joining the military.

While in high school, he was fascinated with the United States Army Junior Reserve Officer Training Corps (JROTC) program in which high school students learn to look sharp, be highly disciplined, goal-oriented, physically fit and develop leadership skills. However, there was no such program in his high school. However, the Army Reserve Officers' Training Corps (ROTC) existed in his college. He saw this as a great opportunity. Unfortunately, he did not qualify for the program. The program required United States citizenship, high school diploma, age between 17 and 27 years, be physically fit and a college grade point average of 2.5. It was the last requirement that he did not meet. Therefore, he went to a US Army recruiting station in a nearby mall. The recruiter, Staff Sergeant Atkinson, always looked sharp, his uniform was always neat and highly pressed. He looked so disciplined, so goal-oriented and so sharp with a very cool haircut called high and tight. Most importantly, his low quarters were always so highly shinning that you could see your teeth while looking at them. At the same time, he was friendly and a great smooth talker.

"I bet he could sell shoes to a snake," Kamal remarked. "I am telling you. This guy will convince the snake to buy not one, but two pairs of shoes and the snake will still feel that this guy did it a favor buying shoes even though it has no feet for the shoes."

"Wow! He should have been a defense attorney," Ray remarked.

Kamal continued, "When you see him in his Class A Army green uniform, driving his official US Army midsize car, you will just be carried away as a young man. You will be saying, 'I want to stand tall and look good like that guy.' You are bound to forget that he is literarily calling you to come and serve and be part of something special which may involve taking a bullet to your chest."

"When I went back home and suggested to my dad that I wanted to join the military, he said that it was a good idea. He felt that it will give me the discipline that he thought I needed. Moreover, the Montgomery GI bill that servicemen were promised would help me pay for college after I completed my tour of duty."

"To me, GI means gastrointestinal, but I realize that people refer to soldiers as GI. What exactly does GI stands for?" Adam inquired.

"I am not completely sure. I have had people called us GI as *Government Inspected* which is probably related to the extensive evaluation the Army will subject you to when you are recruited. The Army really inspects you thoroughly. The other one I have heard is *Government Issued* as in government issued items. I guess this because the Army issues you everything you need including underwear and, well, you are considered to be a property of the US government too."

Kamal continued, "The story was different with Tammy, my step mother. To my surprise, she actually opposed my joining the military. This was a shocker, especially given that we were never really close. I cannot tell you how many times I have reminded her that she should leave me alone. I have yelled at her many times that she is not my mother and she should stop pretending to be my mum. Therefore, I was shocked when she said that she wanted me to be safe. She opined that if I wanted to take some time off from school, then I should get a job instead. According to her, it will be a better choice than going to take a bullet in my chest for a war that I will not know anything about. Her concern was very genuine even though this was peacetime because there was no active declared war going on anywhere that involved United States officially. I pleaded my case and reassured her that there was no ongoing war. However, she was adamant."

"I have been so young and so stupid that I never realized that Tammy had always looked out for me. She had always insisted on my doing house chores with her two daughters on rotational basis. It was not fun at all. I did every house chore such as cooking, vacuuming the house, doing the laundry and dishes. I mean she made me do everything that was supposed to be meant for girls. In addition, I had to take out the trash and cut the grass. At a point, I thought that either she did not know the difference between boys and girls or she was just really mean. She always reminded me of Cinderella's step mother. Like many step children, I also concluded that the synonym for step mother is witch, the wicked type. Every time she made me do whatever I didn't want to do, I had always reminded her that she was not my mother. Every time I got a bad grade, she was hard on me. Every time my teachers complained about me, I would get a proportional retribution at home from Tammy. Honestly, I was always wondering why my father would not defend me and protect me from his witch of a wife. Rather, my father tended to always support his wife by ordering me to wash plates and tidy up my room too. My real mother died in a traffic accident when I was three years old. Later, dad married Tammy and they had my two sisters, Laura and Larissa. They are identical twins, but I could tell them apart. Laura was always unreasonable, but Larissa was always more annoying. In those days, I used to call them "my half-sisters" because I only wanted to recognize their genetic make-up that came from my dad. They used to annoy me back when we were younger saying that if only I wasn't too poor in simple tasks like addition, I would have known that half-sister plus half-sister is equal to full sister."

"I like their mathematics," Adam interjected. "Obviously, they did not like you calling them half-sisters."

"Well, that is true," Kamal agreed. So it was quite touching to see that Tammy was the one advocating for me not to go into the US Army to die. I would have expected her to go to her bed room and be tap dancing that she is finally getting rid of me but that was not the case. Maybe, step mothers are not as evil as stepchildren are wont to believe."

Kamal smiled and remarked, "Tammy is the best mum anybody can have. Her tough love made me understand the difference between mother and mum."

"What do you mean?" Adam asked. "Is mum not the same as mother?" he inquired.

"In my wise neologism, your mother is the one who gave birth to you. However, your mum is the one who raised you. These days, I tend to think of mum as *Mentor Under Matrimony*, that is MUM. That way, if you were raised by your mother, then she is both your mother and your mum," Kamal explained.

"Interesting concept, I must say," Adam opined.

"I have been very close to Tammy since then and I genuinely call her mum with heartfelt gratitude," Kamal concluded.

<u>My Stepmother</u>

I have always regarded her as a witch
Convinced she'll eat me like a sandwich
I couldn't fight the constant itch
To run away from "Tammy the witch"

She consistently made my life miserable
Homework, housework, nothing desirable
Now that I am older and somewhat wiser
Everything has become a lot clearer

I've realized that all she wanted for me
Was to be the best that I could ever be
She wanted me to achieve my full potential
And I needed the training, it was essential

Even if she had given birth to me
She couldn't have done more for me
I am so sorry, please forgive me mum
And I promise to be a much better son

(**Author's note:** This poem is dedicated to all stepmothers and foster mothers of the world, including mine. On behalf of all stepchildren and foster children of the world, I say a heartfelt thank you to all of you.)

"When I dropped out of college after my third semester, I was no better than a person with a high school diploma without any useful marketable skill. Finding gainful employment was no easy task. I did not realize that finding a job would be quite so challenging. Dropping out of any school was not glamorous. I applied to many jobs without success. Then, the heaven seemed to open when I went to The Grocer, a grocery store chain with a branch in my neighborhood. As I finished filling my application, the manager looked at me and informed me that he actually had an immediate opening in sanitation services. The salary was minimum wage with benefits. Although, I was hoping for something better like customer services, cashier, bakery associate, or even as a stock clerk. However, having waited without any job and feeling completely useless at home for 3 weeks, I opted to take the job. As far as I was concerned, it made more sense to keep a job that I do not like than to be jobless. Furthermore, I could always look for another job. I just needed to start something and build my job history."

Kamal shook his head and continued. "Working as a sanitation specialist took away ninety percent of my pride. This was never something I had ever imagined that I would ever do as a job. Calling a person who cleans toilets for a living as a sanitation specialist is like perfuming a pig. Sanitation specialist sounds great when you consider that it means cleaning up after other people. The person who wrote the job designation and job description probably felt that it is a bit more dignifying, but there will never be anything glamorous about it."

Kamal looked at his friends as if he was on a podium advising high school students against dropping out of school waving his index finger as in saying a big no-no, "Cleaning the toilet after other people is not fanciful at all," he surmised. "This is not just about how low the wages are, it is about your wasted potential. If you are at home cleaning your family's toilet like Tammy made me do, you will see it as a necessary duty. However, to be doing that as a twenty-year-old college dropout makes you feel like a total loser. The job itself was not difficult, but thinking of it as a job for young man who used to have big dreams was unbearable. The first day at the job was not bad at all. Nobody spilled anything in the aisle that will make customer service personnel yell, *Clean up in aisle three!*"

Kamal paused, looked at his friends and remarked, "I used to think those customer service guys liked to mess with the cleaning crew when they shout *clean up in aisle ten* loudly over the intercom multiple times in close succession. What I realized was that they do all this rapid response to shield themselves from litigation. The US law is so difficult to comprehend in terms of going overboard sometimes."

"Ray, since you are a lawyer, explain something to me. A person can be in a grocery store, drop a bottle of olive oil either deliberately or accidentally, slip on the oil spill and fall. Yet, this same guy can turn around and sue the store for damages because he fell in the store. Why is that?"

Ray chuckled and said, "That is a great question. Please see my secretary, sign in, give your sixteen-digit credit card number and zip code, and I will be more than happy to answer your question."

"This is an extremely litigious society," Adam remarked. "Things like this are what actually drive up costs of services," he concluded.

"Well," Ray chimed in. "It is not that straightforward. Some of those rules that may be head-scratching were not designed for lawyers to make their boat payments. In actual fact, they were probably promulgated in response to abuses by business owners and to keep a safe environment for all."

"Should the grocery store insist that the guy should pay for the broken bottle of olive oil and pay for the needed sanitation services including the staff effort in cleaning the oil spill, the inconvenience to other shoppers, the loss of revenue to the grocer while dealing with the oil spill, the detergent and water usage expenses as well?" Kamal asked.

"You are sounding like a prosecutor Kamal," Ray observed. "Very good analysis, I must admit. However, like I mentioned earlier, the goal is safety for all."

"I guess you are right," Kamal admitted and continued, "My first day was not bad at all. Most likely, somebody had already done the initial round of sanitation before I arrived. It might have been the evening shift personnel. The following day, I got an opportunity to satisfy my curiosity of knowing what ladies' bathroom looked like."

"Wow!" Ray and Adam shouted in unison almost out of

jealousy. It showed that they had thought about it at some points in their lives too. "What was it like?" Ray asked.

"Honestly, there was nothing to it. It was as disgustingly dirty as the men's bathroom. They also have discarded things that you almost never see in men's bathrooms such as discarded feminine hygiene products and smelly baby diapers. You can use your imagination. The only difference is that they don't have urinals for obvious reasons. Therefore, they have less urine on the floor. So, in case you ever wondered why there seems to always be a long line in ladies' bathrooms at the airports or at conference sites, it is because there are not enough stalls since they have to sit down to, you know, go. Really, it is a stupid curiosity to even think about ladies' bathrooms for a guy," Kamal submitted.

"Despite my disdain for the dirty job, I worked very hard. Nevertheless, I was looking for another job with a lot of vigor. Unfortunately, no other job prospect came my way. By the third week, we got paid. My very first pay! I saw my name on a check for the first time knowing full well that I had worked for it. I had a great sense of accomplishment. The feeling was much more intense that the actual amount on the check. It made me forget the disgusting challenges I endured. It was reminiscent of the popular saying, *Money stinks, but I love the smell of it*. Every time I had to clean some dry goo on the toilet seat, I always felt like quitting the disgusting job. However, when it was payday, all those bad experiences melted away once I got my check. My constant question, *Why am I rotting away here?* became less frequent with time. Soon, weeks rolled into months and my enthusiasm for looking for another job continued to decrease."

He looked at his friends and joked, "It is amazing how much contentment a stupid young man can get from little money when he has no responsibility." Fortunately for me, I got a big jolt to reality with an encounter I had with a little boy and his mother at a checkout lane about four months into the job. The little boy was probably nine or ten years old. His mother was using the Women Infant and Children (WIC) vouchers to pay for the family's grocery. She had a lot of essential food items to pay for such as milk, eggs, orange juice, and beans. Because the food items she picked had to match the approved food items under the program, it took a long time to complete the transactions. Unfortunately, there were many people in the store but few checkout lanes.

Therefore, her grocery transaction took a long time. The checkout line got progressively longer and longer. The mother kept looking at me and was constantly apologizing for taking such a long time since I was the next one in line to pay for an item. Frustration started setting in for the shoppers on the queue at the checkout lane. As the line grew, the embarrassment of the boy increased. The longer the queue grew, the more the mother apologized, the further the son moved away from the mother out of embarrassment. He kept moving away until he started looking at magazines and products that line the passage to the checkout lane to the cashier. It was hard for me to watch and I could not bear it anymore. So, I called the boy and I explained to him not to feel embarrassed that his mother was using vouchers for food. I reminded him that his mother is getting food for him and his sister who was sitting in a pram so that they may have adequate nutrition. I then challenged him that he should rather stay in school and do very well to ensure that he can be in a position to take care of his family in the future. This encounter was a rude awakening for me. I felt like a hypocrite. Here I was, a school dropout, cleaning toilets in a grocery store for a living and literally advising this young boy not to follow my footsteps. If I had married somebody on my salary too, they would also be on food stamps and government subsidies. My son would be embarrassed too. This was an epiphany and I decided to quit the job."

"I guess that the decision to quit the job was not too difficult," Adam opined.

"I just couldn't help imagine the young boy as my son who is embarrassed by his parents' poverty. I am very aware that this government subsidy is a temporary and timely alleviation of suffering for the people who qualify for it. I strongly believe that it is a great program to ensure adequate nutrition for the vulnerable among us. Nonetheless, I would rather be a father who works and makes enough money to feed my dependents. I felt that I could still make that happen and should not resign to fate at the sunrise of my life."

"I totally agree with you," Ray commented. "It is impossible to become rich from asking people for money or to live comfortably from asking people for assistance."

Kamal continued his story that he went home and related what happened to Tammy, his stepmother. He was passionate in his appeal to her. He explained that he could not stand the thought that he could have a son who would be embarrassed because of his failures. He negotiated with his stepmother and she eventually agreed that he could join the Army on two conditions. Number one, he would only serve one tour of active duty which will be approximately 4 years in duration. Number two, he would go back to college once he has finished the service to use his Montgomery GI bill. He agreed to both conditions without hesitation. She then took him to the military enlistment station in College Park, Maryland. He took the initial screening examination which he passed very well. His recruiter, Staff Sergeant William, scheduled him to take the Armed Services Vocational Aptitude Battery (ASVAB) test the following week. In the end, he enlisted in the US Army as a Private First Class (PFC) and his Military Occupation Specialty (MOS) was Air Defense Command, Control, Communicators, Computer Operator.

First, he had to go for basic combat training in Fort Sill, Oklahoma. It was not a thrill at all. Their first task was surviving boredom in the holding platoon. This is where they keep new recruits when they arrive before the next class starts their round of basic combat training. In the holding platoon, all you do is iron your Battle Dress Uniform (BDU) and shine your boots. You will learn how to wax your shoes black and shining using white polish to bring out the shine with a delicate and appropriate touch of water. The goal has always been to be able to see your face and your teeth when you are looking at your boots, especially the tip. The same applies to the low quarters. Everything must be highly shining. For your clothes, you take off lint, you iron them with starch to achieve the military "standing tall and looking good… but without making it too Hollywood." After ten days in the holding platoon, which felt like eternity, the basic training started with the arrival of more privates.

"Why do they refer to recruits as privates?" Adam asked.

"They call all new enlisted recruits privates regardless of their actual military ranks. This is by default because the first three ranks are Private level 1, Private level 2 and Private First Class. However, you do have some guys who finished college and in non-combat military occupation specialty. Those guys come in as Specialists and are referred to as Spec four. This is the same level as a Corporal in a combat specialty. At the beginning, the recruits do not wear their ranks on their uniforms. Therefore, the Drill Sergeants just call everybody privates," Kamal explained.

The first two weeks of Basic Combat Training was hell on earth. It could be aptly described as being yelled at by the drill sergeants for no good reason. Everything was punished with push-ups and more push-ups. Kamal was assigned to Alpha 2nd to 32nd Field Artillery Commandoes. Their third platoon was called "The Steele Warriors." As soon as they got out of the van carrying them from the holding platoon, they met the dreaded Drill Sergeants wearing hats that are similar to those of Thailand rice farmers. They met them without any fanfare. They were yelling for no good reason. The whole environment was tense, and everybody was scared.

"'Private, what is your name?' Drill Sergeant Randy Moreland asked me, and I made a great blunder in my response," Kamal recalled.

"What did you say?" Ray inquired.

"I corrected him. I told him that I was not an ordinary private but a Private First Class. Somehow, the 'First Class' in the rank meant so much to me. The Drill Sergeant was angry beyond description. His face turned red while he was staring at me and I was looking at him. I felt threatened at a point that I decided to break eye contact with him."

"I see. You have an attitude problem, private. We will fill fix it for you!" Drill Sergeant Moreland yelled.

His loud statement to Kamal made more Drill Sergeants swarm to where Kamal was standing. They swarmed like predators converging on their prey. Kamal was now trembling. He started sweating boulders.

"Get on your face!" Drill Sergeant Moreland yelled.

Kamal laid down on the ground with his forehead touching the pavement.

"Not like that, Private Third Class!" Drill Sergeant Moreland yelled again. "Be in front leaning rest position for push up," he clarified.

"That was the beginning of the worst two weeks of my life," Kamal recalled. "So, I assumed the push up position with my hands on the ground, legs straight and back straight without moving."

After a few minutes, he came back yelling again.

"Something better be moving. Either you or the ground!"

After a lot of sweating and numerous appeals of saying *I am sorry Drill Sergeant*, Drill Sergeant Moreland let Kamal get up, stand straight, and drink water from his canteen. Then came the first task for the platoon. The recruits waited with hearts pumping, hands sweating profusely, and many regrets for joining the Army, as the Senior Drill Sergeant in charge of the company prepared to address them. He started pacing from left to right with eyes that shone so bright, they felt as if they were piercing through the souls of the soldiers. This Senior Drill Sergeant was a beast. Senior Drill Sergeant Brandy was a tough guy in all sense of the word. He stood tall at 6 feet 8 inches and weighed about 230 pounds of pure beef. Without saying a word, he would stand in front of some randomly selected poor soldiers who caught his attention and would come close to them like a predator about to devour his prey. He focused his gaze on a few of them and looked straight into their eyes like laser.

"Company, attention!" The Senior Drill Sergeant yelled loud enough to burst eardrums a mile away. He spoke with an unquestionable authority and ordered all the platoons to arrange their rucksacks and sleeping gears in a perfect straight line by squad. Unfortunately, they could not do this satisfactorily. After several rounds of push-ups and repeated attempts to achieve the objectives, the other drill sergeants finally told them that they can only achieve success in the task by working as a team and assigning duties to some members of each squad rather than each soldier standing in place focusing only on his own gear. They did this, and the task was over before you can say Jack Robinson! They learned that teamwork is needed to survive and succeed in carrying out assigned missions.

After the recruits had successfully completed their first mission, Senior Drill Sergeant Brandy started pacing again through the rows. He was a very intimidating guy who was always looking down at most people literarily and figuratively. He was a black belt karate champion and the lead instructor in the military post for the hand to hand combat training. For some unknown reason he took special interest in Kamal—the negative interest type. This was the type of interest that evokes punishment at every opportunity. Some of the other privates felt the drill sergeant picked on Kamal because of his height, since he was also over 6 feet, albeit only 6 feet 2 inches tall.

Kamal was appointed to be the Platoon Guard for the third platoon nicknamed The Steel Warriors. It was obvious to Kamal that he was chosen for this role to make his life more miserable. Whenever some of the soldiers in his platoon were late to the morning drills or formation, the drill sergeants will punish Kamal for the lateness of these soldiers. Drill Sergeant Moreland kept emphasizing that the soldiers that come late would get all the other soldiers killed in combat because they would not arrive at their duty posts early enough to ward off the enemy. All the drill sergeants seemed to enjoy yelling all the time. They never said anything in a normal voice; they only yelled. Furthermore, they make the recruits yell too. It was initially very annoying, but everybody started adjusting after many rounds of push-ups and jumping jacks as punishments. Kamal indeed spent a lot of time in the front leaning rest position, as punishment.

Kamal was surprised about how many physical activities they were made to do virtually every day. By the third week of basic training, they were certified as having some "military bearing" as the softness, weakness, and indiscipline of civilians had now been flushed out of their systems. The drill sergeants became twenty percent less mean. They suddenly transformed from being monsters in US Army uniforms to tough human beings getting their soldier trainees ready for anything that lies ahead in their military career.

Despite this apparent relaxation, no private dares talk back at a drill sergeant. The rule was very simple. "You pay attention. You hear the command. You follow the command." That is the end of the story. What was expected of the soldiers was aptly described by the non-commissioned officer in charge of his platoon, Drill Sergeant Cabamba. He always made it clear, "If I need your opinion, I will give it to you."

The soldiers in the platoon eventually became buddies. All the punishments they all had to endure for the failures of any member of their platoon did the trick. "All for one and one for all" became real for them. This was a testament to the old saying that "pain unites better than pleasure." The collective punishments created a tight bond that was stronger than race, class and the region of the country they all came from. As the drill sergeants often emphasized, "The bullet coming at you does not care who you are and where you are from." It was mandatory for the platoon to chant the platoon anthem whenever a command was given for them to come to attention.

We are the Warriors
We are the warriors
We are made of steel
Our men fight with vigor
Our wrath you'll feel
Hoooooooaaaaah!!!!

The basic rife marksmanship was the most exciting part of basic combat training. Kamal was a terrible shot at the outset. He needed additional time and practice to zero his weapon to ensure that his issued weapon is configured for his own unique accuracy at handling. It was his first time near a gun, which they had to refer to as a weapon, not gun. He was a slow learner in part because he found holding a weapon to be intimidating. He was always anxious whenever he was about to pull the trigger of his M16 A2 rifle and would not hold his breath. His breathing would then change his aim and the trajectory of the bullet every time he shot. Eventually, he got it right after several spit drenching yelling and push up punishments.

As fate would have it, Kamal became one of the best shooters in the platoon. During the shooting examination at the shooting range with pop up targets in Fort Sill, he hit thirty-nine out of forty targets to earn an expert medal. In term of physical fitness, the numerous front leaning rest position punishments actually helped him tremendously. He performed the maximum number of push-ups for his age at the Army Physical Fitness Test (APFT). He also performed the maximum number of sit-ups and completed the two-mile run with more than two minutes to spare while scoring a hundred percent for his age. In total, he scored three hundred points on his fitness test and earned an Army physical fitness patch honor to be worn on his Army physical fitness uniform. Hooooaaahhhh!

On completion of his basic training, he was reassigned to Fort Bliss in El-Paso, Texas for his advanced individual training (AIT). After the completion of his training, his first duty assignment remained at Fort Bliss. After a year in El-Paso, he was reassigned to the 10th Army Air and Missile Defense Command, Kaiserslautern, Germany for one year. He later returned to Fort Bliss for the rest of his military career. His stay in the army was quite uneventful and he made the rank of a Staff Sergeant at the time of his honorable discharge about 4 years later.

Be All You Can Be
The army green
We are good looking when seen
The battle dress uniform
We are tough and we all conform
The fitness test
We are strong and we are the best

This is service to our country
This is our duty to our country
This is honor for me
To be all that I can be
Hooooaaaaahhhh!!!

The skill acquired from training in Fort Sill lasts forever.

He got out of the military and enrolled at the University of Lanham in Maryland to study Accounting. Adjusting to life after the military was not a smooth transition for him. He really missed his routine physical fitness, the group physical activities, and the never-ending competitions with his army buddies. By far, the worst challenge was dealing with civilians. They just don't do what they are supposed to do easily. Worse still, they do not take kindly to yelling at them to do what they ordinarily should have done. He believed that this might have tangentially contributed to his problems with his ex-wife, Kandie.

"You know that the Army issues you everything they think you need. The Army issues you what to wear including socks and underwear. They do not issue you a wife though. I guess, the Army Generals, the Secretary of the Army and the Secretary of Defense do not think you need one," Kamal opined jokingly. "So, if you think you need a wife, you have to go and get one yourself. Unfortunately, you cannot get one in the military Post Exchange supermarket called PX or the commissary grocery store. Getting a wife and staying married is a very complicated mission that the Army never prepares you for. Sadly, you cannot get any hint of it in the military manual smart book as well, as smart as it is supposed to be. So, if you want to screw, you can easily get screwed," Kamal concluded.

"Anyway, I met Kandie in my senior year in college," Kamal recalled. "It was a beautiful Saturday afternoon. We met on our campus during the homecoming Saturday. The main event of the day was the rivalry football game between the University of Lanham and the University of Greenbelt. Kandie was a sophomore at the University of Greenbelt studying political science in preparation to study law. The atmosphere was electric on campus that day and our Buffalo Soldier field was filled to capacity. On paper and by statistics, Lanham Lions should devour the Greenbelt Gobblers, even though both teams had four wins and two losses on the season. Coincidentally, their losses were to Potomac University and the University of Central Anacostia in Washington DC. I initially saw her at the ticketing section with some students from the University of Greenbelt. We were super hyper and shouted, 'Go Lions!' at them, and that our lion will devour their turkey. One of the guys in their contingent had replied that the fact that a lion is supposed to be the king of the jungle does not mean that it will be able to eat a turkey. Then he asked an interesting question, 'Have you ever seen a lion eating a turkey before?' I must say, that was an intriguing question. One of my guys replied to him saying, today is the day when a lion will eat a turkey then.'"

"See you after the final whistle," the Greenbelt student remarked with confidence.

"In a matter of fate, we ended up sitting in the same area of the stadium as these groups of students from the University of Greenbelt," Kamal recalled. "Kandie sat in the row in front of me. She was totally into the game. It was pleasurable to watch."

"What was pleasurable to watch, the game or Kandie?" Adam inquired.

"Both," came the spontaneous response from Kamal. "However, I actually watched the game fifty-five percent, and I watched her forty-five percent. I mean, let us face it. It is hard to ignore a pretty chick who loves football. I couldn't help thinking that this bombshell was rooting for the wrong team. Even though she was not a cheer leader, she surely had a lot of passion for sports. She danced a lot when her team scored, and she was quite good at it. Sometimes, I wished her team would score so that I could see her dance again, but don't tell the Lanham Lion guys that I said so," he advised his friend putting his index finger across his lips to indicate that that information was highly classified.

"You are an interesting dude," Ray remarked. "You were swept off your feet by a chick in less than an hour of watching a football game between two bad teams."

The three of them burst into laughter.

Kamal then retorted, "You ended up in a marriage cage with a dame who criticized you over a muffin. I think my situation was far more romantic and more normal than yours."

Adam then chipped in, "Well, in fairness to both of you, it was all about the projected connection."

"What do you mean?" Ray inquired.

"Sometimes, we just feel that we know that some things will connect and work perfectly regardless of the situation it is put in. Take Nina Totenberg of National Public Radio for example. Is there any sports fan in America who will doubt that she would make a fantastic play by play announcer on the radio for a soccer, football, or baseball game? I mean, think about how she

93

reports the closed-door sessions of those Supreme Court justices in a play-by-play format. Her reporting always sounds like this:

Justice Sotomayor: Global warming is bad for humans and chickens; Justice Roberts: Global warming is also bad for the alligators in Florida; Justice Kennedy: Let's not forget that global warming is very bad for the penguins in Alaska too; Justice Kagan: Global warming will cause drought in many places in the world; Justice Alito: Global warming will cause flooding in many places in the world; Justice Breyer: Global warming is not good for winter; Justice Gorsuch: Global warming is bad in summer; and Justice Ginsburg: Global warming is bad for all inhabitants of earth if there is no world-wide air conditioner to take care of all. Of course, Justice Thomas did not speak."

Adam continued, "You definitely know that it will be easy for her to report like this:

Center Smith snapped the ball to quarterback Carter, pumps fake to the left, fakes a hand off to his running back Randy Dash, throws a long one towards the end zone. It is caught with both feet down by wide receiver Mr. Chase Ball for a 45-yard touchdown."

"Seriously? You can picture her with a microphone and headphones in a booth?" Ray asked.

"Sure. It will be too easy for her," Adam concluded.

Kamal simply shook his head and continued, "I don't know if Nina Totenberg wants to be a play-by-play announcer, but I can tell you that observing Kandie's reaction to the players when they missed a tackle or dropped the ball made it very clear that she understood football. I was quite surprised by this. I had never come across a lady who understood the gridiron that well before. The game was very entertaining with multiple lead changes. I had bragged to her that we were going to beat her team by 10 points when we were up by a touchdown at half time. Unfortunately, her team recovered a fumble and they ran it back for a touchdown against us. The game was tied at thirty points apiece with three minutes to go in the fourth quarter when the game changed. The Greenbelt Gobblers had the ball and were driving into our territory. At the 45-yard line, Kandie somehow called a play to throw the ball down field which the quarterback did, and it resulted into a 45-yard touchdown. It was magical. It was as if the quarterback heard her from the stands, but that was impossible. Her celebratory dance truly rocked me to the beat. She really can dance. Anyway, with the extra point, our team was down by seven points, but we still had one minute and fifty-six seconds to go. I really felt that we could still tie the game, or even go for a two-point conversion to win the game outright without going into overtime since we had all three timeouts. Unfortunately, we could only advance the ball to our own 45-yard line when it became third down and five yards to go with only fifteen seconds remaining in the game after our last time out."

Kandie looked back at me and remarked, "We have this on ice."

"Don't forget about Hail Mary," I responded. "We can still tie the game and go to overtime."

"Not a chance. He is going to throw an interception," she replied.

It was as if our quarterback heard her too. He threw the ball high and it was intercepted in the end zone to end the game."

Kandie looked back at Kamal with *we won, you lost* written boldly on her face. Kamal, sensing that she was about to gloat, decided to strike first.

"Since you are good at predicting things, what do you think I am about to say?"

"I am sorry we lost," she replied.

"No, you're wrong. I was going to say my name is Kamal, what's yours?"

"Kandie," she replied smiling.

Kamal looked puzzled as he had never heard such a name before. "Did you mean "C-A-N-D-Y?"

"Of course, not," she remarked. My name is Kandie, K-A-N-D-I-E. "Why would you assume that my name would be candy?"

"Because you are sweet," Kamal remarked with a smile.

Kandie shook her head with an appreciative smile.

"Well, I could pronounce your name too like the sweet caramel," she joked.

"In that case, the pronunciation would be *ca-ra-mel* not like Kamal," he opined.

"No. The *a* after the *r* is silent. So it is *car-mel* in pronunciation and not *ca-ra-mel*," Kandie countered.

They continued this blabbing as they walked out of the stadium. They exchanged pleasantries and phone numbers. It was as if they had known each other for a long time. They kept in touch and continued their conversations on the phone.

Three weeks later, Kamal was convinced beyond all doubts that he had something special going on with Kandie. She was the lady for him. He could just imagine having a wife who, when he says that he is busy while sitting down in the living room watching a football game, she would truly understand that he is busy. Unlike most women who would wonder, "Why are you saying that you are busy when you are merely sitting down on the sofa and watching TV?" That non-appreciation of a man's commitment to the game is not going to be an issue for this beautiful babe. He was so excited and often daydreamed about him, her, and their first three sons playing touch football in the yard together. That would be a dream home.

However, the road to Kandie's heart was rough and tough. To say it was nerve-racking would be an understatement. She was an activist in the District of Columbia, the protest capital of the world. It was as if she would join a protest to protest against a protest. Kamal, as an Army veteran, learned to follow orders in the Military. Conversely, Kandie, as an activist, protests to defy them. It was uncertain whether they can ever reach a compromise.

"Are you making posters and banners for another protest?" Kamal inquired.

"Yes," Kandie replied.

"I thought you just protested last week," he reminded her.

"Yes, that was to protect sea creatures from oil spill from drilling," she replied.

"And this one?" Kamal asked

"This is to protect dogs from being bred to fight. So, it is a protest against dog fighting. Also, to advocate for felony charges against dogs' owners who leave their dogs in cars during summer heat," she replied chuckling.

"Do you realize that protests do not work in general? Many protesters only end up being arrested and even killed without any effective changes resulting from the protests. This is even more dramatic when the issues affect minorities."

"I am so disappointed in you. Don't you realize that the way to bring about a change is to get involved and let your voice be heard?" Kandie responded.

"Well, I am just afraid every time you go out to protest. I don't want anything bad to happen to you. I love you and my heart is always in my throat until I hear from you that you are back from these protests."

"Oh, Poor baby! Well, I am still going to the protest anyway. Feel free to come and then, maybe, I will allow you to protect me with your big muscles and your military skills," Kandie replied defiantly.

"I started going to rallies and protests with her after this exchange," Kamal concluded.

"And so it was written, another man bites the dust! This is the new definition of compromise in the modern world. It is when the man agrees with the woman," Adam observed.

"What choice did I have?" Kamal asked rhetorically. "I loved her and I did not want to lose her. Besides, I felt I could best protect her when I am with her."

"Yeah right! Mr. Protector. Of course, you were protecting your own interest. Maybe you were afraid that an environmentalist or a vegan will pry her off your claws," Adam teased Kamal.

"Absolutely not! She knows that I am the real man for her. I really love her for reasons that I can't quite explain. So, the first rally we attended together was to protest against financial institutions that prey on the poor with loans that they can't pay back. Now, I was really interested in that because this is a field that I know a thing or two about. I seized the opportunity to let her know that I am in it with her for the long run. I gave a card and a bouquet of flowers when we met to drive to the rally. So, it was nice. It was kind of a rally date."

Loving You
My lovely candy Kandie
Your beauty is stunning
Your character is welcoming
Your words are comforting
Your presence is exhilarating and
Being with you is invigorating
Thank you for being you

I love you.

"And so it was, the lion has turned vegetarian," Kamal chuckled as he recalled attending one protest after the other. Most of what he did was actually standing around watching Kandie shout at the top of her lungs. He was always like a boyfriend bodyguard. Nonetheless, there was always something fun about going to these protests. There were usually lots of people and many of them would not even be able to tell you the nitty-gritty of what the protest was about.

They attended a lot of rallies and protests, such as the protest against big game in Africa to protect the rhinoceroses, lions, elephants. There were many protests about genetically modified food materials, about river contamination from fertilizer run-offs, about recycling plastic bags, about disposing plastic bags, and about increasing funding for development of environmentally friendly biodegradable trash bags. There were just too many rallies and protests. However, one of the most memorable rallies that Kamal attended with Kandie was the one about global warming on Labor Day. The problem was that those who wanted to disprove global warming also staged their counter protest across the street. Occasionally, people carrying contradictory poster will end up in the wrong crowd and will be booed. It was fun to watch for Kamal. People were more civil in their disagreement about the scientific basis of it. People were making emergency posters on site to reply to comments they were reading from opposing crowds. The best of these back-and-forth arguments was between groups of students from Potomac University versus students from the University of Central Anacostia. It seemed that the trigger for this unplanned poster discussion originated from students of University of Central Anacostia when they decided to provide a poster response as a prank.

A Potomac University student carried a poster which read, "Global warming is due to human activities."

The University of Central Anacostia students replied that, "Global warming is due to animal activities, they pass gas."

The Potomac University students responded with, "Stop breeding animals, use less fossil fuels."

The University of Central Anacostia students replied with, "Yes, we agree. Breed more humans, stop using contraceptives."

The Potomac University students responded with, "Your river Anacostia stinks."

This infuriated the University of Central Anacostia students and they replied with, "Your school is Potomac University =

University of Potomac (PUUP = POOP) and it stinks too."

Kamal thought it was funny, but the organizers of the competing rallies did not want any escalation of this lack of civility and they told the students to knock it off.

On their way back from the rally, Kamal informed Kandie that he actually knows the true cause of global warming and that it was a secret. Kandie appealed to him to tell her but he refused. She kept on asking him, using different strategies to pry the answer out of him, but she did not succeed. When she started getting frustrated, he told her that he did not want to tell her when people can hear him as he would not want the information to get out. They boarded the Metropolitan transit train to go for dinner.

Kamal handed Kandie a piece of folded paper and a pen. She opened the paper and read what Kamal had written: *Kandie, I am sorry to break it to you this way, but you are the cause of global warming.*

Kandie looked at him with a you-can't-be-serious look on her face and wanted to respond to this baseless allegation, but Kamal made a gesture for her not to speak by moving his hands over his mouth and pointing that she should write down her response.

Kandie quickly scribbled *you must be joking*, and gave him the paper and pen.

Kamal took it and wrote something in it and gave it back to Kandie.

Kandie read the note, smiled gleefully and gave a friendly slap on Kamal's left shoulder. She then folded the paper and put it in her purse. She gave the pen back to Kamal and tapped him lovingly on the shoulder again. They got off the Metropolitan transit system and stopped by the Alif restaurant, a Mediterranean cuisine by the University of Greenbelt. As they were waiting for their Seekh Kabob order, Kamal read a poem that he had been keeping in his pocket all day to Kandie.

Thoughts for Food

If I am a salad
I will be tasteless without you
Because you will be my dressing
Thank you for enriching me

If I am a pancake
I will be unpalatable without you
Because you will be my syrup
Thank you for sweetening me

If I am a loaf of bread
I will be unenjoyable without you
Because you will be my butter
Thank you for enhancing me

If I am a cereal
I will be unremarkable without you
Because you will be my milk
Thank you for completing me

If I am a mashed potato
I will be uninteresting without you
Because you will be my gravy
Thank you for improving me

If I am a dish of spaghetti
I will be undistinguished without you
Because you will be my meatballs
Thank you for augmenting me

If I am a spread of peanut butter
I will be sour without you
Because you will be my jelly
Thank you for complementing me

If I am a pizza
I will be cheesy and boring without you
Because you will be my toppings
Thank you for perfecting me

I love you so much
I am very hungry for your love
Hope you are having a rewarding Labor Day
Thank you for coming to my life

Tears welled up in Kandie's eyes listening to the poem. She took the poem from him and put it in her purse. When she got back to her dormitory that night, she read the poem over and over again. Then, she remembered the initial note she had taken from Kamal. She looked at it, smiled and remarked, "He is not serious," and she put both notes under her pillow. After a few minutes, she took them out and read them again. She stared at the first note again and remarked, "He is definitely not serious." Kamal had written, *Kandie, it is very true that you caused global warming. You are so beautiful and so hot that the planet is catching a fever. Don't panic, your secret is safe with me. Love, Kamal.*

During the basketball season, they attended many games together. The Lanham Lions faced the Greenbelt Gobblers once. In this locally televised match, the Lions won decisively by a score of seventy-six to fifty. Kamal took this victory to be a consolation for the loss during the football season. The victory was especially sweet because the match took place in the Greenbelt Coliseum.

Loving March Madness
Yes, it is that time of the year
When I can't get enough of my dear
I am not mad about the game
I am crazy in love with a dame

I am not going to dunk
The ball on you
For I am already drunk
From the love from you

However, both teams were not good enough for the National Collegiate Athletic Association (NCAA) tournament nor for the consolation National Invitation Tournament (NIT). It was still fun to talk and discuss the game. Kandie also filled her own NCAA tournament bracket to compete with Kamal. Not too surprisingly, her picks fared better than Kamal's selections because she did better with the upset picks.

You, Me and March Madness
The field starts with sixty-four

101

I know the prize I am going for

Round two has a field of thirty-two
I am still here waiting for you

On they go to sweet sixteen
I wish I had known you since you were sixteen
The schools celebrate the elite eight
I know we are joined together by fate

The states congratulate the final four
I am convinced that together, we'll soar

The nation is transfixed for the final game
I am in awe about you, my lovely dame

The champion gets the trophy and the ring
I can't wait to hold your finger for the ring

Thank you for
Giving me something to dream about

Thank you for
Giving me something to look forward to

Thank you for
Making me long for your love

Thank you for
Being who you are

I love every bit of you

Theirs was a match made in heaven. Sweet lovers they were. Their friends often deliberately spelled their names wrongly as "Candy and Caramel." They were fondly known as "The sweet couple." Although Kamal did not play competitive sports in college, he surely had the looks of a super athlete. He was 6 feet and 2 inches tall and had two hundred and twenty-five pounds of pure beef. He enjoyed physical fitness and weight lifting. Some friends likened his biceps to Mount Kilimanjaro in Africa. Kamal completed his Masters of Business Administration degree from the University of Lanham and took a supervisor job at Washington Metro Sewage and Sanitary Corporation (WMSSC). Kandie completed her Bachelor's degree and took a job working for a congressman on Capitol Hill in Washington DC.

Kamal and Kandie continued their relationship after their college days. They eventually met each other's family members. Kamal could not get Kandie out of his mind. On a six-hour flight from Washington Dulles Airport to San Diego, he made up his mind that he was going to propose marriage and move things along quickly with Kandie. He was tired of being without her even though they have been spending a lot of time together. His thought was interrupted by the announcement over the public-address system by the Echo Airline crew. The announcer remarked that all passengers should return to their seats and fasten their seat belts, as they have started making the final decent into San Diego. Kamal was attending a financial conference as a last-minute substitute for his section Director who could not go due to a major family emergency. So, the Chief Financial Officer tapped Kamal to attend the conference with only a day's notice. He took the opportunity to attend the weekend conference which he felt would be good for his career advancement. Unfortunately, he could not concentrate at the conference. Every girl, lady or woman he met in San Diego reminded him of Kandie. Nothing really interested him. He wrote a note which he planned to give Kandie on his return to the District of Columbia Metro area.

Looking Forwards to Seeing You

I know that you probably don't know
Although I am in San Diego
I would rather be with you

I know that you probably don't know
And you really have little or no idea
How much you mean to me

I know that you probably don't know
That I have been truly blessed

With getting to know you

I know that you probably don't know
That I have been truly comforted
With your coming into my life

I know that you probably don't know
That I see you as my Kandie candy girl
Bright, beautiful, flavorful
And incredibly sweet to the core

What I really do know
Is that I feel very happy
Every time I see you

What I really do know
Is that I feel very joyful
Every time I get a message from you

What I really do know
Is that I am always at ease
Every time I talk to you

What I really do know
Is that I feel elated
Every time I think about you

What I really do know
Is that I TOTALLY REALLY love you
Everything, every day, everywhere and every time

I am truly looking forward to that day
When we will be together
Never to be apart again forever and ever

I love you and I miss you so much

Six months after the San Diego trip, Kamal and Kandie had
an environmentally friendly themed wedding. Life was good,
they couldn't ask for more. However, things took a dramatic turn

just four months after their wedding.

Enjoying the view of San Diego from the convention center.

Part Two: Section Two:
Tempering the Tempest

S o, what happened so soon after the birth of the sweet marriage?" Ray asked.

"I guess, I was impatient. Kandie did not make a quick transition from being a happy-go-lucky lady to a matured married woman quickly enough for me. It was as if she had no clue what married life supposed to be," Kamal replied.

"How so?" Ray inquired further.

"It was as if she wanted to be married without settling down." Kamal continued, "There are certain degree of decorum you would expect from a married woman. For example, four months after our wedding was my birthday. Kandie sent out an email to my friends and co-workers trying to organize a surprise birthday party."

"That does not sound bad to me," Ray remarked.

"No, it was a good idea, but she was reaching out to these respectable people using her email address which was hotlegs22@hotmail.com."

"Okay, what is the point?" Ray asked.

"Did you mean that you really don't see the problem here?" Kamal countered.

"What problem?" Ray asked again looking puzzled.

"Hotlegs22@hotmail.com sounds like an email from a hooker

or a go-go dancer, not from a respectable and responsible wife," Kamal blurted out. "Suffice to say that I heard about the surprise birthday party from these mean guys, but not in a nice way. Their comments were very offensive. I pretty much cancel the party. A part of me felt that I over-reacted, but I just could not put up with their foolishness."

"Lighten up, super soldier! All you needed was to inform her about it in a loving manner. Moreover, does she have hot legs?" Ray asked Kamal in a jovial manner.

"Yes, she has very hot legs… but that is not the point," came the sharp response. "She also dresses way too provocative for a married woman."

"Was she dressing differently when you were all over her like peanut butter and jelly on bread?" Ray inquired.

"But that is different. That was before marriage. After marriage, things are supposed to be different. One should tone things down a bit. You know, a wife should be a bit more conservative. I am telling you, she continued to dress in such a way that was tantamount to making a wanton display of her beauty. The fact that she has it does not mean she should flaunt it. I mean, just because a lady has a killer butt does not mean that she should expose her gentleman's workshop for public view. As far as I am concerned, whether Victoria or Gloria, a lady's secret should remain her top secret. It must be her secret and her husband's secret hide out. In any case, I realized later that I made a mess of the situation. I tried to be better afterwards, and I actually think that I did a better job. I am sure you know that dating a lady and living with her are totally different ball games," Kamal offered.

"Really? I did not realize that," Ray responded with tongue in cheek.

"Anyway, aside from the email situation, things were going great until about a year into our marriage when I quizzed myself about the rationale for postponing having children. I could not come up with a reasonable and acceptable explanation for it. We had been putting it off in anticipation of Kandie going to law school. However, she was working instead. So, the whole thing just stopped making sense to me. I was thirty-six at the time and Kandie was twenty-nine. I thought the time was ripe for us to start having children. If we delayed further, Kandie would turn thirty and even if she went to law school then, she will graduate at thirty-three, maybe spend another year getting settled in a job and by the time we realize it, she will be thirty-five when the chances of having mentally disabled babies increase sharply. Moreover, I wanted to have four or five children. So, it was a big deal to me, but I did not know how to bring up the issue so as not to sound as if I was not concerned about her career interest."

One Saturday morning, Kamal was in a pensive mood. Kandie walked to him noting that he was just staring out of the window without passing any comment. She gently placed her right hand on his left shoulder in a loving manner.

"What are you looking at?" she asked.

"Nothing in particular," he replied without looking at her.

"You may not be looking at anything in particular on the street, but something is obviously bothering you," she responded.

"Well you are right. I am not looking at anything in particular, but I am thinking about something that is very important to me," replied Kamal

"What is it honey?" she asked.

Kamal turned to his wife with an unusual smile that is midway between excitement and fear of rejection. "I think we should have a baby," he suggested.

Kandie withdrew from him after he said this.

"C'mon! Kamal, we discussed this before. We should give ourselves some time, maybe five years. I still want to go to law school," she submitted.

"I know," Kamal replied. "However, we can start building our family and this will not prevent you from going to law school."

"I don't want to delay getting my career on track just for a baby. Besides, when we start having kids, things may start changing for us as a couple," she reasoned.

"I am thirty-six years old now. When exactly do you want us to start trying? When I am forty-one and you are thirty-four?" Kamal asked.

Kandie tried to lighten the mood because she could sense escalation of the discussion in a negative direction. "Don't worry about that Kamal. I have full confidence in you that even at ninety-one, you will still be the macho-man that you are."

"Kamal smiled but it was obvious that he was not happy. The conversation ended there as Kandie went to the kitchen to prepare breakfast. However, over the next four weeks, Kamal kept bringing up the discussion about wanting to have a large family with many children. Kandie felt that he was only trying to get under her skin.

This subliminal tension reached its climax about two months later in the fall. One bright Saturday afternoon, Kandie was having a lower abdominal pain which is common with her when her menstrual period starts. She took some tablets of ibuprofen for her menstrual cramps and decided to lay down on the sofa in the living room. Kamal was watching a very competitive college football game between Ohio State Buckeyes and Michigan Wolverines. Subconsciously, rather than sympathizing with his wife, Kamal remarked, "Another egg wasted!"

On hearing this, Kandie was more furious than she has never been. "You are self-centered and callous!" she yelled at him.

Kamal apologized that he did not mean it that way, but that he could not get his mind off having children now. He had been seeing colleagues bring their children to work, he had seen joyful interactions of families in the park at picnics, and he had been fascinated to see fathers throwing footballs down field for their sons. He just wanted to have similar experiences with his own children.

Kandie just simply ignored him.

A few weeks later, there was a proverbial wind of change. To Kandie, this was an ill wind that did not blow any good. However, to Kamal, this was a wind of opportunity. In a hotly-contested election, Kandie's employer, Congressman Getafix, lost his bid for reelection. Therefore, Kandie was out of job. When she broke the news to Kamal, rather than consoling her, he said that it was an opportunity for them to have a child before she looked for another job. Kandie was visibly shaken and incredibly angry.

"What is wrong with you?" She asked rhetorically. "I lost my job, and all you could think of is having babies."

Kamal kept quiet. A few minutes later, he apologized again but expressed that he truly felt that this was indeed a window of opportunity for them to grow their family.

Kandie remained angry and declared that she was not going to look for any "stupid job" but would rather take the Law School Admission Test (LSAT) and pursue her law degree.

With the baby now versus baby later disagreements raging on between the couple, Kamal started complaining every time about every little thing. It was ridiculous and unbelievable. He complained about Kandie's cooking, he complained about the cleanliness of the house, he complained about the laundry detergent, he complained about the color of the window blinds, he complained about the grass in the lawn and he even complained about the taste of cereal which was the same brand they had always eaten. Kandie maintained her composure, just ignoring all his ranting.

However, when this complaining strategy did not work, Kamal decided to negotiate with Kandie while she was sitting in the bedroom. "What if I take care of the baby while you go to school?" he asked.

"Did you mean, like, you breast feeding the baby?" Kandie replied with a fake laughter. She then put her hand on his shoulder and said, "Come on, Kamal. We will have children, maybe not a boat load. Just wait. Let me finish law school and get my carrier on track. We will have maybe two or three children."

As she was responding, she was looking at herself in the standing mirror of her dresser in the bedroom. The oak finish dresser and mirror set had an elegant finish. It has a touch of class that gives it a vintage look and brings exquisite luxury to the bedroom. Standing in front of it was routinely the final stop for Kandie before she left the house. However, today she wasn't leaving the house. She was just checking herself out. She looked at the picture-perfect right side view of her figure. Then she turned and looked at the view on the left side. Then she turned around with her back to the mirror with her head turned slightly to the right trying to catch a glimpse of what her butt looked like in the mirror.

Kamal knew Kandie was concerned about her looks. So, he remarked in a soft reassuring voice.

"Baby, you will always be my beautiful candy girl and you will make a wonderful mother too."

Kandie appreciated the reassurance with a smile, but rolled her eyeballs as if saying, "Yeah right."

All of a sudden, she busted into hysterical laughter which caught Kamal by surprise.

"What happened?" Kamal inquired. "Did I say something stupid?"

"Come on, Kamal, Of course not! I just recalled an encounter with my mum when my sister and I were talking when we were in high school."

Her sister, Belinda is two years older and was a high school senior when Kandie was a sophomore. Belinda was talking about Frederick, the kicker on the high school football team. Frederick was a very handsome, very brilliant honor roll student who was being very friendly with her.

Kandie continued, "Belinda was talking to me in the living room and we were giggling. Belinda then said that the boys on the football team were nice and they were always having fun. She then remarked that she likes their company. Suddenly mummy burst through the door into the living room like a tornado. Apparently, she had been listening to our conversations while she was cooking dinner in the kitchen. She came to our presence with the big cooking spoon in her hand waving it like a magic wand to make a point to us."

Mummy wore a concerned look and shouted, "Stay away from boys! The only product of their company is babies! Nothing but babies! Babies, do you hear me? Babies! Only babies! Singletons, twins, triplets, babies! Only babies!"

"Yes, Mummy," we replied. "We wanted to laugh so bad considering how funny 'babies, nothing but babies!' sounded to us, but we couldn't laugh for the fear she might be very upset and hit us with the spoon in her hand."

Kandie then looked at Kamal with a gentle nodding of her head and a self-satisfied smirk on her face which indicated mummy was right—*babies, only babies!*

Kamal got the message but shrugged it off saying, "That was a message of a concerned mother to her teenage daughters. She was just trying to guide you to avoid pre-marital encounters that could ruin your lives. That was not about married couples." He moved closer to Kandie and held her hand lovingly saying, "My dear, we are the company, we are supposed to produce babies."

Although Kamal was not interested, Kandie decided to tell him another story of what happened in high school with Ms. Pettiford, their English Literature teacher. She was a nice and arguably the best teacher ever. She later stopped being a beloved teacher who was passionate about literature especially about Shakespeare and became a mean, always angry woman. This terrible transformation occurred when she became pregnant. She became very mean to the students. Her class became a nightmare.

"We were reading Shakespeare's Julius Caesar. When we got to the speech of Mark Antony after the death of Julius Caesar, we were asked to memorize the speech. Our class got in trouble because of the action of Tim the team. Tim was a multitalented and charismatic captain of the basketball team. He was the point guard but was removed from the team because he couldn't guard his mouth. The story was that after the team lost a close game to a less talented rival school, the coach was very upset and addressed the team saying that the players played individual selfish games with each person trying to score. He showed them the statistics that they had few assists in the game and emphasized that there is no *I* in team. Tim then decided out of youthful exuberance to make an inappropriate joke by correcting the coach. He said that the coach was wrong. He told the coach that his name is Tim, T-I-M, and so, that there is *I* in Tim. The coach did not find it funny at all and removed him from the team. Since that day, we all called him Tim the team."

Kandie continued, "During recess one day, Tim decided to draw the pregnant Ms. Pettiford in a typical cartoon style. He drew her in the mocking style that you often see in the newspaper. The drawing had a big head with an uncanny resemblance to Ms. Pettiford, thin arms and legs and a protuberant abdomen indicating her pregnancy. He then drew an arrow pointing to her abdomen and supplied the caption *The evil that men do*. This was obviously with reference to Mark Antony's remark at Julius Caesar's funeral, *Friends Romans, Countrymen... the evil that men do lives after them.* Everybody in the class thought it was a great joke. A female student actually said that, "The babies they produce live after them." We all laughed, but Ms. Pettiford walked in and saw herself. She was overwhelmed with a wintry mix of anger, emotional upset, disgust, and disappointment that was difficult to succinctly characterize. As she tried to speak, she broke into tears. That was when we felt very bad. She went to the school principal's office and filed a complaint and Tim was suspended. The word from the grapevine was that her boyfriend had jilted her after she became pregnant. It is true that men do a lot of evil when they impregnate women and those children do live after them," Kandie concluded.

Kamal felt the story was funny too until Kandie concluded

with her take on it. Therefore, he remarked, "Children are not evil. They are born pure and innocent. It is the parents and the environment that shape and corrupt them. Also, children are comforting, they bear the family name and they are the future. Having children is a wonderful thing. It is necessary for continuity of life. We should... em... em... you know, try and complete our family too by having children."

Kandie did not utter a word. In Kamal's mind, this was a textbook case of the complicatedly simple life of a man versus the simply complicated life of a woman. Eventually, both of them slept with a mile between them on the bed.

Days went by, the house environment was getting colder and colder, but Kandie did not change her mind. Then, Kamal decided that he did not want to use condoms anymore. Kandie replied that in that case, there will be no hanky-panky anymore. This really upset Kamal and he slept on his side of the bed with his back towards Kandie.

While lying down quietly, he was thinking about what to do. Suddenly, he got a brain wave of some sort with a sinister plan. Indeed, the quiet angry man is much worse than an angry man who is speaking his mind. What if he sabotaged the condoms? He shook his head and smiled to himself that it was a great idea. After all, Kandie did not want to be on birth control pills because she does not want to be on artificial hormones. He reminded himself that it only takes a single spermatozoon out of the millions ejaculated to fertilize an egg. Therefore, if he punches a small hole through those condoms in such a way as to create perforations which will not necessarily make the condoms rupture, he may be able to get his Trojan warriors to the battlefield en route to the promised land. He knew that he has to be careful in his execution of his plan to avoid any chances of discovery that the condoms have been tampered with. He has to be very careful to avoid rupture of the condoms because if the condom bursts, Kandie will surely go for plan B.

At the beginning of this *baby now versus not now* standoff, Kandie had jokingly talked about plan B if anything negative should happen.

Kamal recalled asking her, "What is plan B?" and then joked, "Is there a plan A?"

However, to his utmost surprise, Kandie explained that she had attended a ladies' seminar on female empowerment while in

College. The lecturer had explained plan A, plan B, and plan C to them during the segment on reproductive health while urging them to focus on their career.

Kandie had recalled, "According to the lecturer, Plan A is abstinence. This is the safest way to avoid surprises and derailment of career plans. The lecturer had joked that there was only one case in the history of the world that abstinence did not prevent pregnancy. The audience was surprised but somebody at the back of the auditorium got the answer right. She yelled, *In the case of virgin Mary, the mother of Jesus!* This created a stir of agreement among the crowd in appreciation. The lecturer then continued stating, 'Abstinence works as perfect as it can get but if what happened to Mary happens you, I say congratulations to you for being very special.'"

"Of note, Plan A costs nothing!" The lecturer continued. "If you want to eat the forbidden fruit but you don't want it to get stuck in your throat, use contraceptives. This way, you will chew the fruit well before you swallow it. In this case, you will be able to avoid the need for a doctor to help you remove a foreign body from your system. So, if you happened to have unprotected intimate relationship, then go for plan B. This is a medication that you can buy over the counter in your local drug store without prescription, but it costs some precious dollars.

Plan C is the one that lasts forever. That is when C stands for children. In nine months, you will reap what you sow, and they come out crying." Kandi recalled that his made everybody in the audience laugh uncontrollably.

"Of course, I don't need to tell you that plan C costs a lot of money. Unfortunately, they also cost you your shape, your size, your time, your health, and your relationship. However, the most challenging part is that you have to account for them and plan your life around them. So, if you don't feel you are ready, you are not ready for it," Kandie reported the lecturer informing them.

Kamal was very sick to his stomach when he heard this from Kandie. As far as he was concerned, this nonsensical conference obviously polluted the mind of his wife. It was unfortunate that she would not reason that such statements best befit a single woman, not a married woman. He could not understand why his wife did not realize that the responsibility of a single woman is not the same as that of a married woman. A single woman may feel free, but a married woman will surely feel more fulfilled as far as he was concerned.

"Think about it Kandie, this is not a good motivational speaker for happy women," Kamal expressed his opinion out of frustration. "Who was this lecturer anyway?"

"Ada Livespring," Kandie replied.

"Did you mean Ada Livespring, the fifty-nine-year-old talk show host?"

"Yes," Kandie affirmed.

"But she never married," Kamal reminded Kandie

"Yes. She told us that she is married to her career," Kandie explained.

"Exactly my point," Kamal noted. "She is very different from you. Her life trajectory is not the same as yours. This is chalk versus cheese. She is married to her career, but you are married to me. That is a monumental difference, my dear."

"That was her choice," Kandie observed.

"Baby, you can be married to me, be the proud mother of our children and still have a fulfilling career. It is all about appropriate timing and work-life balance. We can do this," Kamal stated almost apologetically. Unfortunately, Kandie could not be swayed to change her position.

At present, Kamal could not think of anything other than the fact he felt justified to sabotage the condoms. Whether, this was just the thinking of a man who wanted his wife to settle down in marriage and build a family or not, this was still the better time for them to have children as far as he was concerned. If that meant that he was being egocentric, so be it. Therefore, he carried out his plan. He used a hand-held puncher to punch a hole in the center of each condom and covered the condom wrapper with a clear tape so that the tampering was not obvious and he could still tear the condom as he ordinarily would.

Kamal then made a fence mending move with Kandie, pretending that he has come around to her point of view. He gave her a beautiful card and took her to a very nice restaurant for dinner.

What I Know and What You Don't Know
What I know
I may appear to be slow

But I know what I know
I know what makes my face glow
It is savoring your love as it flows

<u>What you don't know</u>
Whenever I see you
My heart melts like butter
Whenever you smile at me
My heart flutters
Whenever I talk to you
My tongue stutters
Whenever you frown at me
My whole body shudders
Because to me,
Everything about you matters

I love you and I really care about you.
I am very sorry.

Two months after Kamal hatched his nefarious plan, Kandie felt sick. She thought it was a simple flu, being quite unsuspecting. When her period did not come at the regular time, she attributed it to her not feeling well and losing some weight. It was not until she had missed her period for about two months that she started asking herself if she could be pregnant. She had mentioned to Kamal that she was late, and he had reassured her that it could be because of her flu as she had suggested. Secretly though, he was elated. He was really happy hoping that Kandie would not know until the pregnancy had advanced. The day it occurred to Kandie that she may be pregnant, she dashed out of the house like a person who is possessed. She ran to the drug store chain in the mall nearby. She bought a pregnancy test kit, almost jumping the queue to pay for it, and she hurriedly got out of the store. She went straight to the bathroom on reaching the house. Kamal was nervous. She stayed in the bathroom for a time that felt like eternity.

Suddenly, Kamal was hearing loud banging on the bathroom door as Kandie was screaming. "I can't believe this! I am pregnant! I am pregnant! I am pregnant!"

Kamal went to the bathroom and knocked on the door for Kandie to open the door. She opened the door sobbing. It was at this point that Kamal felt bad. Now, it dawned on him that he had betrayed the trust of his loving wife. However, he was not sure what he should do. Should he tell her the truth? Should he just take it that the Almighty has answered his prayers and keep his mouth shut? He chose the latter. With a fake concerned look on his face, he put his arms around his wife hugging her as if he was really consoling her and muttered, "It was an act of God! After all, no child can come to this world without the leave of God," he remarked.

Kandie kept asking loudly, "How did this happen?" and she wept even more. "I am planning to take my Law School Admission Test (LSAT) examination in 6 weeks, what am I going to do now?"

"You will be okay my dear. I have full confidence in you that you will ace the examination in spite of the pregnancy," Kamal reassured her.

That night felt longer than 24 hours. She could not sleep. She could only toss and turn in bed. She was in shock. Kamal was very supportive, and he cooked dinner for her and encouraged her to eat. In the morning, Kandie told Kamal that she is considering having an abortion.

"What?" Kamal shouted in disbelief. "Why on earth would you even let that cross your mind?" We both know that we want children," he continued. "We only differed in when the baby should come. I preferred now, you preferred later, but there is no doubt that we want to have children at some point in time. Please do not bring Roe versus Wade into our home. You can take your LSAT and still go to law school. As far as I know, pregnancy is not a contraindication for admission to law school."

Kandie remained unconvinced. She stated that she does not want to be struggling with too many things at the same time. She does not want to be struggling with herself, Kamal, her school work and a baby at the same time. It would be too much. When Kamal's reassurance seemed to be falling on deaf ears, he decided to call Kandie's mother over the phone to solicit her support to make Kandie change her mind. He explained to her that Kandie is pregnant, but she is threatening to have an abortion. He appealed to her to call her daughter to discourage her from aborting their first child.

In this panic mode, Kamal also contacted Belinda, Kandie's

sister who had been married for four years and did not have any children yet. In actual fact, she was undergoing treatment for presumed infertility. She and her husband have spent a lot of money out of pocket on conventional medicine and alternative therapies. At that point in time, they were considering in-vitro fertilization which could cost thousands of dollars in out of pocket expenses.

Eventually, it was the tearful Belinda who got through to Kandie and convinced her to keep her baby. She told her that if she still feels negative about the baby after birth or feels that the baby is interfering with her law school at any time, she will be happy to look after the baby for her. This really touched Kandie and she changed her mind about having an abortion. Nonetheless, she was not happy. She passed her LSAT but decided to wait another year before applying to law school. Kamal Junior was born on eleventh day of July at 11:45 a.m., weighing 8 pounds 3 ounces. Kamal was elated. Some of their families and friends even remarked that the boy looked like him but more handsome because of the good looks that he got from his mother.

Two weeks after Kamal Junior was born, the guilty conscience was over whelming for Kamal. This was more so when Kamal Junior was crying and Kandie was making every effort to keep up with breast feeding, trying to keep the house clean, cook, and maintain the normalcy they had before the baby was born. Kamal stepped up to the plate and helped at home more that he had ever done. The home training from his stepmother finally paid off. He relieved Kandie of any housework that he could do instead. He strived extra hard so that she could concentrate on the baby and get some rest. He started doing the laundry, cleaning the house, going grocery shopping and even cooking for the house on a regular basis. In fact, one day after cooking dinner, he asked Kandie about the correct way of announcing dinner formally.

"Is it more appropriate to say dinner is ready or dinner is served?" Kamal asked Kandie.

"It is okay. Don't worry about it. Thank you for doing the cooking," Kandie replied.

"You are welcome. Hope you had some rest, but I really want to know. This will be a way to boost my homemaking grade point average," Kamal responded.

"I don't think that it matters," Kandie answered.

"I was thinking that dinner is ready will mean the food is done but it is still in the pot or in the oven depending on what has been prepared. This will indicate to those invited that the food is ready for whenever they chose to eat. However, dinner is served will connote that the food has been dished on the table and everything is set. This will indicate that those invited to dinner should stop whatever they are doing and come to the dining table. Is that correct?" Kamal asked.

"Honey," Kandie replied with a forced smile while looking so tired, "If the cooking was like you did it yesterday, I think the most appropriate announcement will be *dinner is burnt*!"

Kandie and Kamal burst into laughter, which woke Kamal Junior up and he started crying again, causing more frustration for Kandie.

When Kamal junior became two months old, things were settling down in the house. Kandie has become more energetic and Kamal remained a very helpful father at home. Unfortunately, his guilty conscience about the conception of Kamal Junior continued to haunt him. Kamal decided to come clean with Kandie on how she had conceived. He bought a blank card and wrote a poem of apology.

(**Author's note: Poll for readers:** Should he tell her? Now; Later; or Never. Please go to blissfulgardenz.com)

I am Very Sorry
I have an empty feeling
From doing a lot of thinking
I am so sorry for what I have done
I really wish it could be undone

I may not know
If my words of apology
Will ever be enough

I may not know
If many cards expressing my sorrow
Will ever be sufficient

I may not know

If any gift in the world
Will adequately convey the message

I may not know
If my facial expression
Will be able to reveal my sincere remorse

I may not know
If my tear laden eyes
Will ever demonstrate how sad I am

I may not know
If you will ever forgive and forget

But what I do know
Is that my life is sullen with regrets

I am very sorry
I love you

Kamal gave Kandie the card, a bouquet of roses and a box of Belgian chocolate. With genuine tear laden eyes, he informed her that he had sabotaged the condoms. He apologized for his misdeed.

Kandie was shocked to her bone marrow. "You did this to me deliberately?" she yelled at him.

All Kamal could muster was, "I am very sorry."

In a hysterical outburst, she threw the flower at Kamal and picked Kamal Junior from his baby cot. She was about to walk out of the apartment when she remembered that the temperature outside was ninety-nine degrees Fahrenheit. It was a bad idea to take a baby out in such weather. So, she returned into the house, went into the bedroom and locked the door behind her. She was crying uncontrollably. Kamal became even more confused and did not know what to do. Now, he felt that it was probably a really bad idea to have confessed about what he did.

After giving her some time, Kamal entered the bedroom using his key. He tried to comfort her saying, "I am very sorry." He tried to touch her shoulder. She yelled at him to leave her alone. Her shout was so loud that Kamal Junior who was sleeping woke up suddenly and started crying. This only increased the annoyance of Kandie. After some minutes of pleading without making any headway, Kamal left the bedroom. In the evening, Kandie put the baby on the bed in Kamal's usual sleeping area rather than his cot. Kamal decided to pass the night on the couch in the living room trying to give peace a chance.

The following day, Kamal continued to apologize to Kandie who was still too angry to listen to him. The problem dragged on for two weeks without resolution. By this time, Kandie had stopped cooking for him and would not eat whatever he cooked. She did not want him near her and the baby. Kamal tried another strategy of giving her a handwritten card with an expensive but very beautiful diamond bracelet which he charged on his credit card. He was hopeful that this should begin the process of normalizing their relationship.

I Miss You

It has been a very difficult time
Two weeks and two days
That my world turned upside down
I really miss you and
I am very sorry

The major problem for me
Is that I don't know what to do
I am truly sorry
I really feel empty without you and
I am very sorry

Without you
I feel like a clown without smiles
I feel like a day without the sun
I feel like a night without the moon
I feel like king without his queen and
I am very sorry

I love you
Always have, always will
I am very sorry

To his utmost surprise, Kandie rejected the expensive bracelet. She read the card and then tore it in Kamal's presence and threw it in the trash container in the bathroom.

"I don't want your card. I don't want your gift. I don't want to see you," Kandie shouted.

"I said that I am sorry. What more do you want?" Kamal asked rhetorically in annoyance.

"What I want? I will tell you what I want, you self-centered bigot. I want my life back. I want my life back! Can you give it back to me? Can you give it back to me? You are a wicked soul!" she yelled at him.

Kamal shook his head in utter disbelief.

Unfortunately, the friction got progressively worse and their marriage began to crack. Kamal became more frustrated. He called Kandie's mother to intervene. She did and appealed to her daughter to forgive her husband. After all, he did it for love. Unfortunately, this did not make Kandie warm up to her husband. Even the appeal from Belinda also fell on deaf ears. Kandie and Kamal started drifting apart. Kamal started coming home late as the home environment seemed to have lost its joy. Kandie's attention focused exclusively on her baby. They were no better than hostile roommates. Eight months after Kamal Junior was born, Kandie, who had been working part time in a manufacturing company, decided to switch jobs. She took a full-time position with a communication company in Old Town Alexandria in Virginia very close to the Nation's Capital. She felt more financially secured.

The hostility in the house continued to grow until one Sunday evening. Kandie took a hundred-dollar bill from Kamal's wallet without asking his permission. He held her hand trying to retrieve it back. Kandie called emergency number 911 alleging that Kamal was trying to beat her. The dispatcher sent two police officers, a male and a female, to their apartment. When the police officers arrived at the apartment, they found Kamal watching television in the living room. They interviewed both of them. He told them that Kandie started the whole problem and that she still has his money. Kandie did not deny this, but kept telling the officers that she is the victim because Kamal held her hand. The police officers gave Kamal three choices. He could leave the house and go and stay with a friend or go to a hotel or they could arrest him and take him to the police station. Kamal was flabbergasted. It seemed that the police officers were only interested in whether he touched her hand or not. The police officers did not seem to care about the facts of their dispute. What was unfolding in his presence seemed to be a default position that the man is guilty no matter what the truth is. While he was still thinking about these bad choices, the female police officer, Detective Melissa William passed a suggestive remark.

"I am sure that your wife will soon be complaining that her left shoulder hurts. It could be a rotator cuff tear. I had one of those before from my boyfriend and I know how much that can hurt. It is going to be a lot of problem for you and you will be arrested."

"Did my wife tell you that her shoulder hurts?" Kamal asked.

"Not yet, but she may," Detective William replied.

"I really do not understand this. Nobody is addressing the fact that she started this problem. She is the one who went to take my money from my wallet and she has not even given it back," Kamal protested.

Rather than addressing Kamal's query, the male detective, Detective Manny Minefield who is now feeling rushed, spoke bluntly to Kamal. He said, "Sir, I do not like to do avoidable paperwork. So, why not do the rest of the world a favor and just leave the house so that peace can reign. The way I see it, you can come with us to the station or you can go to another place of your choice. What is it going to be?"

Kamal shook his head in amazement. He had been given a *take it or we will take you* choice. He definitely did not want to be arrested. He thought to himself that in an attempt not to be labeled as being guilty of misogyny, the society has moved to misandry. "Is misandry a continuum from feminism?" He asked himself without an answer.

Playing a Mime

Love is cool, only when it is good
Otherwise it is worse than rotten food

So, when she is really annoying
And you're really close to fighting
Try your best not to talk

But you should rather take a walk

Instead of going postal or running amok
Cool down, calm down and take stock
For it is better to look stupid playing a mime
Than to go to jail for an avoidable crime

Kamal felt betrayed as he left the house wondering where to go. "What we need is a balance in our society. We need to recognize gender roles that benefit the society at large. We do not benefit from subjugating any segment of the society. This is unfair," he said to himself. He felt the system was unfair to him because he is a man. He later called a friend and crashed with him, sleeping on his couch. He made efforts to contact Kandie many times, but she did not pick his calls and did not reply to his numerous text messages. Kamal felt he needed a cool-off time from Kandie too. So, he stayed with his friend for five days. On Friday afternoon, he went back to his apartment. However, his key could not open the door. He later realized that Kandie had changed the lock. That was why his key could no longer open the door. This was surely extreme. He was shocked. It was unbelievable. He waited around for a few minutes, resisting the urge to break the door.

He waited for about thirty minutes while knocking the door intermittently. He did not know whether Kandie was inside the apartment, but was just not interested in opening the door for him. He went to the apartment leasing office to complain. To his surprise, they said that they got a petition from Kandie that she needed to change the lock to the apartment to protect her and her son from Kamal. She had shown them a restraining order from the court to that effect. This was a rude shock to Kamal and he returned to the front of the apartment. He waited at the door for Kandie to arrive. About forty-five minutes later, Kandie arrived at the door with Kamal Junior in a baby stroller. Kamal approached them trying not to show his anger.

"Good evening, baby," he said as he approached her trying to help her with her bag.

"Don't baby me. Go away from me and my son," she snarled at him.

"But he is my son too," Kamal countered in a harsh tone,

losing his cool.

"He does not need you in his life. Go away!" She shouted.

"Why are you talking like this? Why are you doing this to me?" He asked.

She brushed him aside as she opened the door. He forced his way into the apartment after her. Kandie took her phone threatening to call 911 again. Kamal then appealed to her not to call the cops. Realizing that this was a very difficult situation for him, he asked her to give him thirty minutes for him to take his stuff out of the apartment and she agreed. With tears rolling down his cheeks in disbelief, he packed a suitcase with some of his clothes and his valuable documents, and he went back to his friend.

A few days later, he got himself another one-bedroom apartment and tried to move on with his life. All his attempts to reconcile with Kandie proved abortive. She did not want to communicate with him. There were no replies to his numerous text messages. His phone calls always went directly into her voicemail and he never got a call back. It appeared that his calls were blocked by Kandie. All his efforts to engage Kandie's family to talk to her on his behalf were unsuccessful.

About a year later, Kandie and Kamal were set to meet in court for divorce proceedings. Kamal was anxious about the end of his marriage. Things had been tough being separated from his love and his son. He was anxious about seeing Kandie. He was not sure what to expect or what might happen. However, he was looking forward to seeing Kamal Junior for the first time in a long time. He has missed a lot of his developmental milestones. As far as he was concerned, he has missed everything important about his son. He was so excited to at least see him, probably hold him in his arms. Then he started wondering if his son would cry if he approaches him since he is going to appear to him as a complete stranger.

Disappointingly, Kandie came to the court house alone. She did not bring Kamal Junior to the court. Kamal was devastated. This was too much to bear. However, the worst was yet to come. The deliberations were brutal. Kamal represented himself. He did not think that he needed a lawyer; after all, this was a simple divorce. Or so he thought. How wrong he was!

Kandie came to the court house with a simple black dress. It was nothing fanciful. She was wearing a pair of dorky eye glasses. Kamal was surprised because he knows that Kandie's eye sight was a perfect 20/20 and that she does not wear glasses except sunshade glasses. "Why is she wearing glasses?" he asked himself.

When the court session started, it became apparent that Kandie wanted to appear like a simple woman who was being oppressed and abused by her husband. She really dressed for the occasion. It was well played. It was brutal. Kamal versus Kandie case felt like Kamal versus the Department of Justice, the County Police Department, the local sheriff, the postmaster, the Metropolitan bus driver, the grocer, the trash collector and everybody on the planet not named Kamal Brown. He felt that the entire world was against him.

Beginning with the opening statement, Kandie's lawyer laid down a dossier about Kamal with a lot of emphasis on his military experience. It sounded nice and Kamal's mind wandered away. He started reflecting on his life with Kandie since they met at that football game in Buffalo Soldier field in College. He could not help it, a part of him still loved her. He played back his relationship with Kandie in his mind before everything went bad. Indeed, they had a lot of memorable moments together. However, the one that stood out for him was the day he proposed to her. He remembered it as if it was yesterday. It was the third week of January. It was a cold Monday afternoon. It was a holiday. It was the Martin Luther King Junior birthday holiday.

Kandie had invited him to attend a rally to honor Martin Luther King, Junior's message of peace, cooperation and justice for mankind. The rally had many notable speakers with a lot of references to the iconic *I Have a Dream* speech by Martin Luther King, Junior. After the event, they stopped for lunch at a local diner, and Kamal told Kandie that he had his own dream speech. She became curious and eager to hear it. For Kandie, it was interesting to hear Kamal try his own version of the dream speech. The waiter came to their table at this very time thereby interrupting them. He asked them if they were ready to place their orders. They quickly asked for orange juice and randomly picked the first dish they saw on the menu. Kamal tried to remember the food; whether it was chicken, beef, lamb or shrimp. He could not remember. The food was not all that important to him then, and neither was it important to know what it was now. He remembered taking a paper on which he had scribbled some words and began to read, "I have my dream."

The Dream

I have my dream
I dream of that day
When a suitor is judged not by the size of his wallet
But by the size of his heart
Hopefully, not causing a heart attack

I have my dream
I can't help dreaming of that day
When a suitor is judged not by his bank statement
But by the statement made by his character
Hopefully, not restricted to 140 characters

I have my dream
I really dream of that day
When as a suitor you'll let me make my case
As per why you should be by my side
So that we can go together to the seaside

I have my dream
Let's face it, you are my dream
And I am hoping you will come to pass
And be the wife that I have always dreamt of.
If my love for you is a dream
Darling, I certainly don't want to wake up.

When he finished, tears of joy were rolling down the cheeks of Kandie who was trying to fight her emotions and surprisingly, a lot of people in the restaurant responded with "Aaawwwww!" Kamal and Kandie were so lost in their world that they did not realize that the people in the diner had been listening to his recital, including the waiter who had not even left to bring them the orange juice. Kamal brought out a ring and asked Kandie to marry him. Kandie was shocked. It really took her by surprise. She took the ring and said, "Yes," and every busybody in the diner applauded.

Everybody has a dream, but we celebrate the dream of Martin Luther King, Jr.

Kamal was still quietly reveling in his recall of the joy he felt that day, which was only matched by the incredible joy he experienced when Kamal Junior was born. It was hard to believe that he was in court to divorce the same Kandie. "What ever happened to Candy and Caramel, the sweet couple?" he asked himself without an answer.

Kamal came back to reality as the lawyer was finishing his speech that Kamal was a well-trained soldier in the United States Army. The lawyer even shared with the judge that Kamal's favorite Army jingle cadence song was "The Army Colors":

> "The Army colors
> The colors are red
> To show the world
> That blood we've shed."

The lawyer sang the cadence three times without reading the other segments of the song. It was as if he was trying to emphasize the shedding of blood component of the song.

Out of the blue, the lawyer made a petition for the sole custody of Kamal Junior.

"What!" Kamal interjected, not believing his ears and jumping to his feet. If his world was already on the ground from the divorce he is going through, denying him custody of his only child was putting him underground.

He spoke out in a loud voice, "No way!" to which the

presiding Judge Fairchild ordered him to behave well and not interject or interrupt during the proceedings. The judge then addressed Kandie and her lawyer.

"Why do you want to sole custody?"

"My husband is abusive," Kandie replied.

"How is he abusive?" Judge Fairchild asked.

"He is verbally abusive, and he is a trained solider," Kandie replied.

"Did he ever hit you?" the judge inquired.

"Yes. He held my hand before causing me pain in my shoulder and I called 911. The dispatcher sent two cops to our home. They did not charge him for assault and battery or domestic violence but they asked him to leave the house. So, your honor, I am afraid for my life and my poor baby because he may be angry one day, and he may beat me and my baby," Kandie responded in tears, a performance worthy of an Oscar Award.

At this point, her lawyer, Attorney Pinocchioto jumped up from his seat and addressed the judge.

"Your honor, the fact that he has not beaten her mercilessly previously does not mean that he won't."

The judge was still not convinced, and he remarked, "Why should we take what he has not done, use it against him, and thereby, deny him access to his son?"

"Your honor, sir, should we wait until he has done so? We know, sir. We know that we do not want to wait until he has done so. We will be too late, your honor. We will be too late to intervene and the consequences of this will be fatal. We have to remember that he was trained to be a killer. He is a trained killer."

Kamal was exasperated. He wondered how he went from being a person who proudly served his beloved country to being branded as a trained killer that everybody should be afraid of. This is even more troubling since he never served in combat.

The lawyer continued his argument. "Should we wait and see? Should we stand by and do nothing until he uses the effective killing skills that our military taught him on this ordinary helpless, defenseless poor young woman and her innocent, helpless defenseless child?"

Kamal could not fathom what made these people be a

hundred percent convinced that he is going to kill his wife and son in cold blood. It all seemed like a bad dream. It was just that this was reality playing out in the courtroom. This was no dream at all. This was shameful.

Suddenly, the lawyer pointed to Kamal and shouted. "Look at him. Look at how strong he is. Look at those heavy biceps. Look at his pectoralis chest muscles. Look at his broad shoulders. How long do you think it will take him to break her neck if he is angry?"

Then, in a remorseful tone, he concluded his speech. "She will not stand a chance to call 911."

Kamal sank in his chair. He wanted to shout at this stupid lawyer that "It is a lie!" However, if he did that, it will appear confirmatory that he has anger problems. He was in shock.

The judge seemed to have heard enough and ruled in favor of Kandie.

Kamal made his appeal to the judge recalling that Kandie did not want the baby in the first place. He was the one who wanted a child. He even emphasized that Kandie wanted to abort the baby. He mentioned that he was denied his rights to his son and that this will only deny the son his right to his father. All his reasoning fell on deaf ears. The judge awarded sole custody to Kandie and set the money for alimony and child support to be paid by Kamal.

Kamal was devastated. This is injustice. Immediately the case was completed and ruled upon by the judge; Kandie dealt Kamal with a really low blow. In a move that is akin to the winners of the Super Bowl taking out *We are the champion* tee shirts after the game is over and the confetti has started falling, Kandie took out a tee shirt from her purse and wore it over her dress. It was a callous move. She added the proverbial salt to Kamal's injury, as her tee shirt read, "I am wild and free!"

This was the worst day of Kamal's life. It was bad enough that he has permanently lost Kandie, the lady he loved, but to also lose his only child was too much to bear.

Broken beyond repair.

Part Two: Section Three:
Seeing Clearly in Hindsight

After the show of shame in court, the custody battle was now officially over. In fact, it was not a battle at all, not even a wimpy fight as Kamal did not stand any chance at all. The justice system has been orchestrated to work against men. Women know it and they exploit it. Kamal was dejected. "Taxation without representation" seems more desirable than what has been wrongfully and callously imposed on him by the judicial system that defaults to take care of women in wanton disregard for men. Now, he is being made to pay money to raise a child he is not allowed to see and to pay for upkeep of a woman he cannot go near. This is oppression. He felt the judicial system failed him. Now, his son will grow up without his father simply because the mother wanted it that way. "Do fathers have any right in this land of milk and honey?" he asked himself.

This ordeal was too much for Kamal to bear, especially when as an accountant he balances his check book and always noted how much of his income goes to Kandie on a monthly basis. His coworkers in the office noticed that things have not been going well for Kamal, and his productivity suffered. One year later, he was still struggling with his emotions. He really felt that Kandie, Kandie's family and the judicial system were unjust with him. One bright Friday afternoon, the Personnel Director called him to his office and told Kamal that his performance review showed that his productivity index had fallen to eighty-five percent of the previous year. He sympathized with him, but told him to get whatever help he needed so that his problem will not get compounded by unemployment.

Kamal went home that day and felt the worst that he had ever been in his life. He had always thought of himself as a tough guy. Apparently, tough guys can have emotional crises too. Suddenly, it occurred to him that perhaps he should take a vacation and go somewhere he has never been as a way of jumpstarting his life. The finalist cities for his rejuvenation vacation were Orlando, Miami, Cancun, Puerto Rico, and Hawaii. In the end, he chose Hawaii because he would be in the airplane for the longest time. He booked Echo airline. Unfortunately, in recent times, Echo airline had been an echo of its glory days. Customers complain very frequently about the performance of the airline. The flights are often delayed, with too many double bookings and subpar in-flight amenities during flight. As far as many travelers were concerned, Echo airline was in its own custom-built echo chamber. The airline only hears itself and not its customers. Five days before Kamal was to travel, there was a major change in Echo airlines and the Chief Executive Officer was fired. The new CEO promised to institute a customer first operation and bring back the heydays of Echo airline.

The day of the beginning of his head-clearing vacation finally came. Unfortunately, his cab ride was complicated by a fender bender between his cab driver and another motorist on highway I-295 before they could join the Southwest Freeway towards the Ronald Reagan National Airport. The other motorist insisted on waiting for the police rather than just exchanging insurance information. By the time it was all sorted out, Kamal barely made it to the airport on time. Fortunately, he had no luggage to check in and already had his boarding pass. Just for today only, he wished that his Echo airline flight was delayed as usual. His heart got a heavy dose of adrenaline as he looked up at the monitor and identified the information about the gate for departure and status of his flight. For the first time in a long time with Echo airlines, he saw *On Time* and almost immediately, it changed to *Boarding* while Kamal was still looking at the monitor. He ran as if he was trying to break the land speed record towards the security gate dragging his rolling duffel bag. With his heart racing, he finally made it to the security check point with only ten minutes remaining for boarding. He tried to be quick with the standard processes. He emptied his pockets, took out his laptop and quickly removed his wristwatch, belt, and shoes. He assumed the position for body scan routine. He also took off his wedding ring which he was still wearing despite being divorced for over a year. Unfortunately, in this mad rush to catch his flight to Seattle he dropped his wedding ring and did not realize it. He made it just in time, but the plane was already airborne when he realized that he did not have the ring in his possession. The flight to Seattle was otherwise uneventful. He decided to wait at the gate for the connecting flight to Honolulu, given the wait time of one hour and thirty minutes. Unfortunately, the flight to Honolulu was overbooked. Therefore, the airline official offered a five-hundred dollar ($500) gift certificate for any five travelers who were willing to give up their seats and continue their journey the following day. Their flight will be guaranteed for the following day. Kamal took the offer. After all, he was not going for any urgent matter. He was given a five-hundred dollar flight certificate which he could redeem within twelve months. In addition, he was given vouchers for three meals and an airport hotel voucher for one night. When he arrived at The Executive Hotel, he was pleasantly surprised how beautiful the hotel is. The environment was very neat, and the attendants were warm. The check-in line was not long. There were three receptionists attending to customers. They were all pleasant. They were constantly smiling which could have made you wonder if they were advertising a new brand of toothpaste. Kamal's turn came to be checked into a hotel room. He approached the hotel's receptionist to redeem his voucher. He was quite impressed by the cheerfulness of the receptionist. Her badge read, "Bonita."

"Checking in sir?" she asked in a very warm tone.

She had the most sonorous voice Kamal had ever heard. To Kamal, she sounded more like, *I am truly pleased to see you*, and *you are safe with me*. Her smile was so pleasant that Kamal felt a rush of adrenaline.

(**Author's note**: Actually it was testosterone but let us stay with adrenaline. It sounds better and less creepy).

Kamal became flushed and sweaty with his heart galloping away like a horse in The Kentucky Derby. That is what adrenaline does to you. He tried to regain his composure, but his voice betrayed him and he stammered to say, "Y-y-yes!" A voice in his head encouraged him to cancel the trip to Hawaii and just spend his vacation in this hotel in Seattle just to see this lady again. There was something about her that was pulling his heart to her like a magnet. He just could not put a finger on what it was.

"My flight was rescheduled by Echo airline till tomorrow. I am here to keep you company... er... er... er, I mean that I am supposed to stay here today and fly out tomorrow," he stuttered as he handed over the voucher to Bonita.

"I am sorry to hear that your flight was cancelled," she sympathized with him.

"Oh no, it is okay." Kamal responded. "Every cloud has a silver lining. At least, it has given me the opportunity to meet you," he asserted with a broad smile.

He spoke with such a radiant smile with a loving tone of appreciation that would truly convince anyone that "it is truly an ill-wind that blows nobody any good. This was no ill wind at all."

"That is so nice of you." Bonita replied as she started typing on her computer keyboard to redeem the voucher, check hotel suite availability, and assign a room for Kamal.

Kamal could not help noticing that Bonita was not wearing a wedding ring. Somehow, he convinced himself to keep chatting with her.

"So, am I going to get a pent house?" He asked in a very friendly and familiar tone.

"Awww!" Bonita remarked as she looked up from her computer screen to make eye contact with Kamal. "We sold out of those," she added with a facial expression that reflects empathy for a missed opportunity.

The spontaneity of the response and how cool she was answering such a rhetorical question was so impressive that Kamal could not help chuckling. He tried to avoid showing that he was laughing but could not hold it and he laughed out loud. Bonita laughed too.

"Yeah right," Kamal remarked. "I know what you were thinking. You were probably saying to this to yourself, "Seriously? Pent house on cheapskate airline's voucher?"

"No sir," replied Bonita, shaking her head. "Echo airline is our respectable customer and we treat all our guests with utmost respect to make sure that they have a pleasant and memorable stay with us."

Kamal was convinced that this was not the customer service job at work. Rather, this was simply a very nice person who is working as customer service personnel.

Kamal smiled and said, "Thank you Bonita. I really needed that laughter."

"You are welcome sir," Bonita responded with a smile.

She then gave him his keys to room 831 and informed him of his rights and entitlements including the location of the elevators, the hours of the complimentary hot breakfast, the location of the business center, the fitness center and the hours of operation of the swimming pool. However, the only thing Kamal heard was 831. Everything else she said was blah, blah, blah in a sweet, loving manner. He was consumed by the thought of the significance of 831.

The Special Number
There are numbers
And there are numbers
The first number is eight
Makes you feel great
The middle number is three
Helps you to feel free
The last number is one
Reminds you that she's the one

Eight three one is a statement
A statement as a testament
An opinion with a sentiment
An expression in wonderment

It will change your life
It is worthy of the strive
It will make you feel alive
It is happiness that has arrived

This thought is revealed in eight letters
This feeling is conveyed in three words

This emotion is expressed with one meaning.

I LOVE YOU.

Kamal took the key cards, thanked Bonita and headed to his room. He could not stop thinking about her. Is this love or is this lust? He certainly did not know the answer but he didn't care. The only thing that matter was that he loves the vibe from her and he wanted it to last forever.

He changed into his gym clothes and headed back to the lobby of the hotel. At the reception desk he saw Bonita again. He asked her for the direction to the fitness center. Well, he did not pay attention when she told him a few minutes earlier. He was busy observing how beautiful she is and how great her voice sounded. Anyway, Bonita informed him again without even mentioning that she told him the same thing only a few minutes earlier.

In the gym he tried to burn off the love energy he has just consumed. For one hour and twenty minutes he spent in the fitness center he could not stop thinking about Bonita. On his way back from the fitness center, he stopped by the reception desk to catch a glimpse of Bonita again. Since there were no customers waiting, he approached the reception desk and started talking to her. He revealed to her that he is a divorcee and gave her an ultra-short summary of his life story and how he ended up in Seattle. He was unsure why he told his life story to a stranger he met only about two hours previously. It was just that there was...

Something Special About Her
Something welcoming about her
Something calming about her
Something comforting about her
Something relaxing about her
Something pacifying about her
Something mollifying about her
Something placating about her
Something soothing about her
Something special about her

His thoughts went berserk about her. *Surely, something seemed special about this sweet stranger who is soft and soothing to somebody seeking succor.* "Bonita Orozco is my dream wife," Kamal said to himself over and over again. For a moment, he became convinced that it would be a good idea to cancel his Honolulu trip and spend his time in Seattle instead so as to keep seeing Bonita. In the end, Kamal left Seattle as scheduled and continued his trip to Honolulu. While vacationing in Honolulu, he called Bonita multiple times on the phone.

Kamal was physically on the beach in Hawaii, but his heart was in Seattle.

Kamal looked at Ray and remarked, "It is amazing how a person can enter your life and make you forget all your sorrow. It is interesting how you can get lost in the arms of someone who loves you, who gets you, who knows you and who is there for you. Talking to Bonita on the phone left me foaming in the mouth with excitement, seeing her melted me like a candle, and just being around her made everything else in the world disappear. When I returned home from my vacation, I knew that I had to see her again."

"I have never felt like that before. Yes, I loved Kandie before, but this was truly special. She makes me feel so good all the time. Her name, Bonita, means beautiful in Spanish. She is so pleasing to the eyes, that she makes her name beautiful. Despite her attractiveness, her beauty is less of an attraction than her character. She has a calming demeanor about her. Her voice is so soft, it will disarm you. Her smile will make you smile. I once told her that her smile is what made me realize what *infectious smile* means."

"For four straight weekends, I flew to Seattle just to see her, but I did not stay at the hotel where she worked the last two times. We became friends but I wanted more. Why not? She was the light at the end of my dark tunnel. She was my lady of light. I sent her a card and had a basket of goodies delivered to her by Amazon. For the first time in a long time, I felt alive. Kamal was back," Kamal recounted.

The Dark Tunnel

I barely slept every night
Not due to being in a state of fright
But because of longing for delight
The delight is you, my lady of light

Every morning, I long to see you
Every afternoon, I wish to catch a glimpse of you
Every evening, I can't stop thinking about you
Every night, I feel so pathetic missing you

Loving you is always a delight
Your love is always in my sight
Craving you is what I endure every night
Missing you is sadness for me, day and night

Hoping to see the bright light
At the end of this dark tunnel
Light! Light!! Bright light!!!

"Our relationship continues to grow exponentially. We connected even more when she told me that her family came from Juarez in Mexico and live in El-Paso, Texas. I told her that I was stationed in El-Paso in Fort Bliss during my military service days but that Juarez was off-limit. Therefore, I never visited the city. Unfortunately, I had limited interactions off the military base and did not learn Spanish at all except for very few words including *hola*. I knew enough psychology to realize that I needed to make a lot of effort to connect with Bonita and her family. I should make more effort to learn the Spanish language and know more about the Spanish culture."

"Our love continued to move leaps and bounds. Bonita finished her course in childhood education from the University of Seattle. After about a year, I decided to propose marriage to her. I wrote my intention in English and had it translated into Spanish. The translation was done by my co-worker, Jimena, who I fondly refer to as The Bolivian Flower. I then copied the Spanish poem into a blank card. It was my way of showing her that I am ready to assimilate into her rich Latina heritage."

Peace in My Life
Oxygen saves lives
Water saves lives
Blood saves lives
Love saves lives

Oxygen is stronger than vacuum
Water is stronger than oxygen
Blood is stronger than water
Love is stronger than blood

Being with you is my drive
For your acceptance do I strive
Please enhance peace in my life
By becoming my lovely wife
I love you

Translated version (in Spanish)

Paz en Mi Vida
El oxigeno salva vidas
El agua salva vidas
La sangre salva vidas
El amor salva vidas

El oxigeno es mas fuerte que el vacio
El agua es mas fuerte que el oxigeno

La sangre es mas fuerte que el agua
El amor es mas fuerte que la sangre

Estar contigo es mi motivacion
Yo lucho por tu aceptacion
Por favor aumenta la paz en mi vida
Y conviertete en mi amada esposa
Te amo

"Fortunately for me and the rest of the world, she accepted," Kamal concluded.

"Why do you think it was fortunate for the world that she accepted your marriage proposal?" Ray asked with a fake puzzled expression on his face.

"The whole world is better with a happy Kamal in it. Trust me, I know that very well," came the quick response from Kamal. I made it very clear to her that I am prepared to live my life with her by my side.

<u>Next Step</u>
Loving you is strangely different, a mystique
I probably shouldn't be surprised, you're unique
You have a wonderful and beautiful stature
And you are kind, nice and gentle by nature

Marrying you is adopting a new culture
Don't worry baby, it will be my pleasure
I will flourish like bacteria in culture
For my love for you is without measure

Baby, let me take you home to my people
And I am so ready to meet your people
My love, open your heart to me
My dear, share your island with me
I love you

Jimena was on hand to help me translate it again.

<u>Proximo Paso</u>
Amarte a tie es extranamente diferente, un misterio

Probablemente no deberia estar sorprendido, eres unica
Tienes una maravillosa y hermosa figura
Y eres Buena, amable y gentil por naturaleza

Casarme contigo es aceptar una nueva cultura
No te preocupes bebe, lo hago con amor
Voy a florecar como bacteria en cultura
Porque mi amor por ti no tiene medidas

Nena, dejame levarte a mi casa con mi gente
Y estoy muy listo para conocer tu gente
Mi amor, abre tu Corazon a mi
Mi carino, comparte tu isla conmigo
Te amo

"I travelled home with Bonita to meet my dad, Tammy, and my sisters. They treated Bonita as if she was their missing daughter. Larissa actually asked her why she did not come sooner to her brother's life."

"Interesting question. So, how did she reply?" Adam inquired.

"Of course, she could only respond with a smile. There is no real answer for such a question," Kamal responded. "We arranged for me to also meet her parents over the Memorial Day weekend in El-Paso. It was a sort of homecoming for me. I had not been back to El-Paso since I left the United States Army. While there, I stopped by my last duty station briefly. I did not know anybody there anymore. Everybody I knew back then had rotated out to other places or made other life changes."

"My meeting with Bonita's family was remarkable. They were very warm hosts. Her father Mr. Jose Orozco must be the nicest man on earth. He is a very hardworking man who owns a landscaping business. Her mother Michelle works in a grocery store. Bonita is the eldest child. Her two brothers, Eric and Diego, came home from college. I spent the whole day with the family. I really felt at home."

"We got married in a simple wedding about three months later. I was pinching myself to ensure that I wasn't dreaming. She was all I ever wanted. She made me realize that a home is a where you feel the safest. It is a pity that I had to go to work from Monday to Friday. I always wanted to just be with her at home. I really felt the difference between a house and a home."

"And what is the difference?" Adam asked.

I will love you forever.

"When you finish paying your mortgage, it becomes your home, otherwise it is your house. This is because if you fail to make the needed payment on time, the lender will foreclose it," Ray explained.

"That may be true, but that was not the difference that I expressed to my lovely Bonita," Kamal clarified.

"What then did you tell her, Mr. Buddy Love?" Ray queried.

Between a House and a Home

Being at home and
Being in a house
Are not the same thing
Not just in spelling

House is the fence against intruders
Home is the protective custody of your arms
House is the energy efficient window

Home is sharing a meal with you for energy
House is the roof to shield from heat
Home is dancing with you to the beat
House is the plumbing for water to flow
Home is holding your hand for love to flow

My love, whether we live in a big house
Or simply getting by in a small hole
My darling, I will always be at home… with you!

I love you and I want to be with you forever and ever

"I told Bonita that I will always be home with her no matter where we live," Kamal explained.

"Wow! You fell this deep in love from just eating tacos? Oh my lord, I need some Mexican tacos too," Ray remarked in jest.

"Of course, this is not just about food. Although she is an outstanding cook, she is just a wonderful person. I was hurting so bad from what Kandie did to my psychology, I thought that I would never love again. Boy, I am so glad to be wrong," Kamal concluded.

"Are you sure that Bonita doesn't put love spices in your apple juice? This may be the reason why she is the apple of your eyes," Ray joked.

"I hope those love spices keep coming then. It is really special when you are truly in love." Kamal opined. "There was a time, I went to a conference in McCormick Place in Chicago. The conference was from Monday morning to Thursday afternoon. I arrived on Sunday evening. I was already feeling home sick by Monday afternoon. I couldn't wait for the conference to be over so that I could go home to Bonita. I went to the post office close to my hotel and I mailed her a card with a hand-written poem that I composed for her. Even though I knew that she may not even get the card before I returned home, writing the card to her had a significant calming effect on me."

What My Heart Feels
It is peace
The tranquility from you taking care of my heart
It is joy

The happiness that you are the one I want
It is sweet
The taste you leave in my mouth all the time
It is honey
The rich golden color of indescribable bliss
It is special
The greatness that comes with your humility
It is love
The feeling that only my heart can convey
It is pain
The emptiness of your being away from me
I really miss you my love.

"Funny thing was that she actually got the card the day before I left Chicago. Our United States Postal Service personnel should pat themselves on the back. It came to her as a great surprise which she really appreciated. That really made me so happy that I was still able to pull an unexpected love move on her," Kamal reported.

"How do you get to function and work if you are so attached to her apron and you miss her so much?" Ray asked.

"I am just happy with her. It is hard to explain. I mean, I have gotten three speeding tickets going home to see Bonita after finishing from work. On two of those occasions I called her on my way from work. She was such a darling to talk to and I just became in a hurry to get home. So, I increased my speed only to see the cops tailing me on Richmond Highway. After this happened twice, I stopped calling her when I am driving home."

"Wow! And the third time?" Adam asked

"I was just thinking about some of the conversations that we have had and I just became impatient to see her," Kamal explained.

"This is serious. Most men get speeding tickets running away from their wives or running towards girlfriends. Yours is the opposite," Adam observed.

"I feel for those men," Kamal observed. "That is not the end of the story of the Chicago trip."

"So, what did you do? Did you get her a piece of the moon?" Adam inquired.

"That would be nice, but I do not have the resources for that; so, I did the next best thing. I bought a blank card and a box of chocolate for her at O'Hare airport. The brand of chocolate was Chicago Chocolate: Love whirlwind from the windy city. The packaging was well designed and beautiful. Of course, I did not know how the chocolate would taste, but the confidence exuded by the proprietor of the Chocolate Company in his description of his product was just too wonderful to ignore."

"What did he say?" Adam interjected.

"It was something like—this chocolate will cause love whirlwind on her taste buds and a whirlwind of love in her heart," Kamal recalled.

"I am impressed," Adam submitted.

Trying to show off a little bit, Kamal adjusted the collar of his shirt moving them forward with a broad smile and declared that he is a man for the ladies.

Adam and Ray looked at each other and chuckled. It was obvious that they were saying to themselves, "Yeah right! Say that to Kandie who flattened you out like pancake."

With his ego having received a big boost, Kamal continued his tale of his triumphant return home from his Chicago expedition. "However, the most surprising move I had was what I was hand-carrying."

"Let me guess. A pair of shake-it-for-me high-heel shoes," Ray answered mockingly.

"No. I bought a deep-dish pizza from a pizzeria in Magnificent Mile and carried it with me all the way to the District of Columbia," Kamal stated.

"You must be kidding!" Ray exclaimed out of surprise.

"That was exactly what the lady sitting next to me on the airplane said too when she saw it. The difference was she was moved and thought Bonita was lucky to have me. Like I said, I am a man for the ladies," Kamal remarked adjusting his collar forward again.

"Cut it out, Mr. Buddy Love! Why did you come home from Chicago with a deep dish pizza anyway," Ray inquired.

"Everytime I talked to Bonita while in Chicago, she was always asking me if I had eaten, if the food was good, if I had enough sleep et cetera. Believe me, if she could be sending me her cooked meals by firing them to me using a giant catapult, I am sure that she would have done so. There is nothing in this world that compares to having a beautiful wife who loves and cares about you."

"Aww!" Adam remarked trying to sound like a studio audience at the filming of a sitcom.

Kamal continued, "I had to constantly tell her that the food is great in Chicago, I tried to describe the deep-dish pizza but I didn't do a good job. So, I decided to surprise her with it. After all, a taste is better than a million pictures."

"If we may ask your majesty, the honorable King of infatuation, what did you write in the airport card?" Ray asked in jest.

"This is not an infatuation but true love," Kamal countered.

"Okay. Whatever you say," Ray resigned.

Being Away from You
When we are both at home
And I am sitting down on a sofa
And I stretched my hand to the right
And I stretched my hand to the left
And I did not touch you
This is being away from you; grade one
And I don't like it

When we are both at home
And I am lying down on the bed
And I roll to my right
And I roll to my left
And I did not touch
This is being away from you; grade two
And I detest it

When you are somewhere
And I am anywhere
And I cannot see you in person
And I cannot hear you in person
This is being away from you; grade three
And I hate it
Let us just say, I am happy to be on my way home

"Honestly, my life was going great until six months ago. While at work, I got a call from a number that I did not recognize. I did not pick it up, but the caller called back immediately. So, I picked it up. To my surprise, it was Kandie. I was shocked."

"What did she want?" Adam asked being surprised.

"She was crying. She said that Junior was ill, and she had brought him to the emergency department of Children's Regional Hospital. My heart jumped into my mouth. I asked her what happened, and she told me that he had cough and fever and suddenly developed some breathing problems. I immediately jumped into my car and drove straight to the hospital," Kamal related.

"Sorry to hear that. Hope he is okay now," Adam expressed concern.

"He is doing great. He has fully recovered from the pneumonia, but they asked us to always watch out for episodic breathing problems. They are suspecting that he may have an underlying asthma. The boy is doing great. I am the one who is not doing great."

"What happened?" Ray inquired.

"I got to the pediatric emergency department and quickly made my way to the emergency room where Junior was being treated. As soon as Kandie saw me, she got off her chair and hugged me while crying. It was a bit awkward considering her triumphant show of shame in the court room. However, I felt it was because of the fact that Junior was ill and she was overwhelmed with emotion. I passively hugged her back and patted her back to reassure her that he will be fine while she was crying on my shoulders. The problem was Kandie wanted more than that."

"How so?" Ray asked

"Well, we were together in the emergency room for about five hours before they finally moved Junior to the ward on the fourth floor. I had to call Bonita to let her know where I was. I just couldn't leave Kandie alone with Junior in the emergency room at that time. Unfortunately, that meant spending five hours alone with her and an additional hour in the ward before I left for home. It also meant going back and forth to the hospital to see Junior while Kandie was there. He was admitted for three days. The good part was that I got to spend some time with my son, the bad part was that I had to spend some time with his mother."

"So, you guys were catching up?" Adam asked jokingly.

Kamal sighed, indicating that something went wrong.

"Please don't tell me that you guys reconnected," Adam asked almost freaking out.

"That was the beginning of the problem. We did not really reconnect per se at that time. However, we had a lot of discussions ranging from recollecting our time together in college, those sport events, et cetera. Eventually, we discussed what was going on in our lives. I told her that I am happily married. She asked me her name and I informed her that her name is Bonita, she is Hispanic, and that her family is from Mexico. I actually showed her Bonita's picture from my wallet."

"Kandie remarked that Bonita is very beautiful. I was pleasantly surprised by the response from Kandie. I became confused as per what I should say next. Should I simply say thank you and keep quiet or does courtesy demand that I should say something nice about her too? I think that was the point where I made a blunder," Kamal related.

"What blunder?" Ray asked

"I thanked her, but added that she looked beautiful too," Kamal explained. "This actually made her smile, but what she said afterwards caught me off guard."

"What would that be? Stop paying the child support?" Ray asked in jest.

"You know that hell will probably freeze over first before that will happen. No, she praised me and apologized for how she treated me," Kamal recalled.

"Really?" Ray and Adam asked in unison.

"Yes. It was unbelievable," Kamal recalled and continued to relate his discussion with Kandie.

"You are a nice guy, Kamal. I am sorry that I just didn't see it that way back then," Kandie commented.

"Well, such is life. Things do happen. Glad to see that you are doing okay too," Kamal responded.

"Not really," Kandie stated.

"Why? What happened?" Kamal inquired.

"After we broke up…"

"You mean after you treated me badly," Kamal interjected unable to control himself.

"I am sorry," Kandie reiterated in a very soft tone and paused for a few seconds. It appeared as if she had an emotional reaction of some sort or probably remembered something that made tears well up in her eyes.

"I was moved. Seeing her fight her tears made me pity her, but because I did not know what to say, I kept quiet," Kamal recalled.

"After the divorce, I guess things were okay initially. Junior was doing okay. Everything was okay," Kandie stated while desperately trying to find the right words to keep the conversation going.

It was awkward for Kamal. He did not know what to say. He started wondering if he was supposed to ask her if she had remarried or not too. Then, it occurred to him that it was actually better for him to ask and if she had remarried, he could stop paying spousal support for her. Emboldened by this realization, Kamal proceeded to ask Kandie about her love life.

"So, have you remarried?" Kamal asked her, trying to show some concern.

"No, I haven't," Kandie responded with a disappointing tone. Kamal was disappointed too albeit for a different reason.

"I haven't found the right guy yet," she concluded.

"Oh, I see. In due time, the right guy will come along," Kamal sympathized.

"It is not that I didn't try," Kandie continued. "About six months after our divorce, I met Julian through a friend. He is a musician and plays a guitar. After about four months, he asked if he could move in with us and I said okay. He is originally from Canada and he was thirty-eight years old then. He will always tell me that he is destined to be the next Justin Bieber. At first, it was funny. He called himself a stay home dad and that he is practicing his music so that he can hit it big on the world stage. He played a few gigs here and there, but nothing fruitful. We had a major fall out about five months later when he started smoking his cigarettes inside the apartment. I could no longer put up with his nonsense. I called him 'Juliana' and expressed my frustration about him. He was really angry at that. Which man in his right masculine mind wants to be a stay home dad when he can go out to work and make things better for his family? It is ridiculous. I can even understand if the man is the better caregiver for a disabled child or something like that. In our case, how is he a stay home dad when Junior is not at home but in daycare or school? He does not contribute anything of significance to our finances. I told him that the only person who probably believes in his music talent will be his mum, and that will be because she is deaf."

"Is his mum deaf?" Kamal asked just out of curiosity.

"I don't know, but she had to be if she thinks her son has any music talent," Kandie countered.

"Wow! You really hit this poor guy below the belt," Kamal remarked.

"I kicked him out. I was just tired of putting up with men like him," Kandie explained.

"There were others?" Kamal asked.

"They were just a bunch of players who were nothing but vultures looking for their next prey. Somehow, there are so many useless men out there who prey on single mothers. They pretend as if they care, but they don't. They are merely looking for their next victim," Kandie remarked in anger.

Kamal just kept quiet, even though he felt vindicated in his mind. He tried to offer some comforting words.

"Things will be okay," Kamal remarked, trying to reassure her.

On the day that Kamal Junior was discharged from the hospital, Kamal went to see his son and got there just before the paperwork for discharge was completed. He hugged his son passionately and the sight of father and son love truly moved Kandie.

"Thank you very much for coming and for your support, Kamal," Kandie stated.

"Well, it is my duty. After all, he is my son," Kamal commented.

"I was thinking of calling my lawyer so that we can petition the judge for us to have joint custody arrangement so that you can mentor your son and be the father that you wanted to be for him," Kandie submitted.

Kamal was ecstatic on hearing this from Kandie. He agreed that it would be a great move on her part. Soon afterwards, the paperwork was completed and they both had joint custody of their son.

"I am not sure what happened and how things moved so fast, because I started seeing Junior and Kandie more often," Kamal continued.

Adam cleared his throat with a chuckle. "Oh no, please don't confirm what I am thinking."

"What are you thinking?" Kamal inquired.

"I am not saying it. Please continue," Adam related.

"It appeared that Kandie had become a lot calmer. Her attitude towards me had changed to that of respect. It felt great and awkward at the same time," Kamal concluded.

Premature Sunset

Under normal circumstances
Under ideal conditions
It is a beautiful sight
It is a wonderful delight

The color of the setting sun
The view of the fading rays
The warmth of the dissipating heat
The magic of the disappearing shadow

This is very different
This is a sad event
The sun should not set at noon
The night should not come too soon

Many things we did regret
Many things we want to forget
Many things we did were mean
Many things we did not mean

My eyes are clearer now
My sight is better now
My head is clearer now
My judgment is better now

Let's stop the bleeding today
Let's wash our sorrow away
Let's end the grief
Let's turn a new leaf

"Did you tell Bonita about your meetings with Kandie?" Adam asked with a mountain of concern written on his face.

"Yes and No," Kamal replied.

"What does that mean?" Adam queried.

"Yes, because I always informed her that I was going to see Junior. No, because I never put any emphasis that I will see Kandie too. I am sure that it was implied," Kamal submitted.

"So, have you started exchanging forbidden pleasantries with Kandie?" Adam raised the question with a lot of concern.

"No. I was saved by the bell," Kamal submitted with a sigh of relief.

"What did you mean?" Ray asked.

"It happened about a month ago. After I had started going to see Junior..." "His mum, you mean?" Adam interrupted him.

"C'mon, Doc! I went to see Junior and seeing the mum happened. Anyway, about a month ago, rather than meeting at a park or public places as we usually do, she asked me to come by the apartment instead. She told me that her car was in the mechanic shop for repairs. The plan was for me to pick them up. We will watch a Disney movie with Junior and I will drop them off at home afterwards. When we came back, we went into her apartment. She asked me to stay, that she wanted to make me my favorite meal. She invited me to join her in the kitchen as we typically did in the good old days. She wanted to prepare spaghetti and meatballs. She reminded me how we both agreed that she is the spaghetti, being all over the place and I am the meatballs being in strategic places. She told me that she had not cooked it in years. Come to think about it now, somehow, she had all the ingredients ready in the kitchen when we got there. Maybe it was just a coincidence," Kamal opined.

Adam and Ray looked at each other in disbelief as per Kamal's naivety regarding the encounter with Kandie as he had related it so far.

"Coincidence my foot! Are you kidding me? Seriously? You really think that it was a coincidence that she got you into her apartment to prepare your favorite meal that she had not cooked in years?" Adam queried.

"Relax man!" Ray chimed in to calm Adam. "Continue Kamal, I am listening with rapt attention."

Kamal continued. "We started cooking together and somehow, one discussion led to another leading us to be having nostalgia for the good old days. I am not sure who started it, but we started singing our favorite songs. We started dancing together while Junior was watching Tom and Jerry cartoon. One thing led to another, we embraced each other and had a passionate kiss."

"Oh my God!" Adam exclaimed.

"It was at that point that somebody rang the doorbell. I felt as if I had been in a trance and the doorbell just woke me up. Kandie was raving mad when the doorbell rang. She told me to ignore it, but I insisted that we answer it since we were not expecting anybody. She went to the door and it turned out to be one of the employees of the apartment complex. The maintenance guy had been called by the occupants of the opposite apartment 201C for a leaky faucet and he had just inadvertently rang the wrong doorbell of apartment 201D. The short interval that Kandie went to answer the door was what it took to bring me back to my senses. It dawned on me that Kandie is not my wife but my son's mother. My wife is Bonita and she is at home where I live, not where I am. When Kandie got back to the kitchen, my senses had returned from whatever seductive land it went to. I told her that I was sorry for everything that had just happened, but I needed to leave. She said that it was okay and that I should calm down. Furthermore, she wanted me to still stay for the meal. I insisted on leaving but I could see disappointment written on her face in bold letters. When I got into my car, I needed a moment to process what had just happened and what did not happen. I asked myself repeatedly, *Kamal what were you thinking?*"

"That is the problem. You were not thinking!" Adam interjected again.

"Suddenly, being saved by the bell took a whole new meaning for me. When I got home, I did not know what to tell Bonita. She asked me how Junior was, and I replied that he is doing great and left it at that. My guilty conscience still pricks me here and there since then and makes me feel awful," Kamal related and sighed in dejection.

"You were really lucky to have escaped by the skin of your teeth. She set you up and you fell for it. Are you planning to tell Bonita?" Adam inquired.

"Absolutely not!" Ray interrupted. "Bonita is the lady in your life, your model wife, who has successfully made you get speeding tickets going home not once, not twice, but three times. My friend, do not ruin what is going on well in your life with honesty that is not needed."

"But Bonita has been wonderful to him," Adam recalled.

"Exactly why he should keep his mouth shut," Ray defended his position. He then looked at Kamal who by now had his elbows on the table and his head was resting in his hands. "Dude, you did not score a home run. Okay, you made it to the first base, but no real harm done yet. Let us keep it that way. Lest I forget, was it not your telling the truth when you did not have to that cost you your marriage to Kandie in the first place? Why on earth would you want to make the same blunder with Bonita?"

"By the way, what happened after you left? Did Kandie reach out to you again?" Adam inquired.

"Yes, she did. She asked me when I would like to stop by her apartment to see Junior again," Kamal recalled.

"It is a trap!" Adam exclaimed.

"We know it is a trap, but he still needs to be involved in the life of his son," Ray reasoned.

"These days, she will put Junior on the phone and he will talk to me saying things like *Daddy, when are you coming? Daddy, I miss you.* I told her that I will come soon, but she will want me to make a commitment as per when that will be. She reminded me that our join custody allowed me to have him on alternate weekends too. I really want to be involved with my son, but I want to avoid being involved with the mother. I am not a saint you know," Kamal submitted.

"Nobody is expecting you to be a saint. The fact is that it is impossible to escape when a beautiful woman is targeting you," Ray concluded.

"How about you discussing with Bonita? You should mention that you will love for her to meet Junior? You can make it sound to her that you will be happy for her to do so, if it is okay with her. That way, Kandie can bring Junior over to your house. Kandie can then meet Bonita and realize that you have moved on and you are happy. That may let her know that there is no need to reopen that deep wound she caused you," Adam suggested.

"What deep wound are you referring to?" Ray asked Adam. "He already kissed her passionately from his own narration. The wound has healed without any scar! This is the reality!"

Kamal did not say anything. It was as if his mind has wandered away out of the Milky Way into a different galaxy. After a brief period of awkward silence, Ray spoke again.

"Big man, I think I am going to agree with Adam's

suggestion. Get Bonita on your side almost like your bodyguard even though she won't know it. Find a way to go with her anytime you are meeting Kandie, and bring your son home to spend some weekends with you. You have to avoid being alone with Kandie at all cost without letting Bonita be suspicious."

The three friends agreed that this was the best-case scenario.

Adam asked Kamal for his Public Service Announcement.

(**Author's note:** Kamal's Public Service Announcement is a song written by the author.)

Public Service Announcement from Kamal

Woman, Not Woe to Man
I may be getting old
But never forgot what I was told
Women are our love
They are not our lord

Chorus
It is not right
It ain't right
It will never be right
Woman, not woe to man

We should treat women well
But men don't have to go to hell
We should be nice to women
But we should not ice the men

Chorus
It is not right
It ain't right
It will never be right
Woman, not woe to man

How women are treated can make you dizzy
But we should not overcorrect and drive men crazy
This is not just for marriage sanctity
It is to prevent us from ruining the society

Chorus
It is not right
It ain't right
It will never be right
Woman, not woe to man

You are the one for me
Baby, look at me
You are one of a kind
Baby, what's on your mind?

We don't need to bury our heads in sand
We can surely do this hand in hand
We love our daughters, wives, and mothers
Why not the same for our sons, husbands, and fathers?

Chorus
It is not right
It ain't right
It will never be right
Woman, not woe to man

Between her rights and his responsibility
There has got to be civility and sensibility
Tell me if this makes any sense to you
Share with me if this feels like you

Chorus
It is not right
It ain't right
It will never be right
Woman, not woe to man

He worked very hard and spent a lot of money
Because he is convinced he has a great honey
She is pretty and brainy, a total package
Only for it to end after two years of marriage

Huh!

She claimed that she made a big mistake
That he does not seem to have what it takes
She claimed that he is a piece of trash
Just because he doesn't have enough of cash

Chorus
It is not right
It ain't right
It will never be right
Woman, not woe to man

She wore clothes for a statement of fashion
While the man sinks in debt in a very big mansion
She is a yo-yo, traveling up and down
While the man is lonely, always looking down

Yet, the judge did what's hard to imagine
He decided to kill the man's spirit and his engine
He gave her the car, the house and the bank
And didn't care if the man dies of hunger pangs

Chorus
It is not right
It ain't right
It will never be right
Woman, not woe to man
You are the one for me
Baby, look at me
You are one of a kind
Baby, what's on your mind?

It is difficult, but we have a task
It is hard but we have got to ask
What is the future for men in the land of milk and honey?
When you spend the money but you don't get the honey?

Huh!
Woman, not woe to man!

It is terrible, not funny
Woman, not woe to man!!

It is gloomy, not sunny
Woman, not woe to man!!!

Huh!
Woman, not woe to man!!!!

Huh!
Woman, not woe to man!!!!

Interjection

Ray tried to cut a piece of his rib eye steak when he had a sudden jerky motion and he lost control of his knife. He tried to adjust his grip to catch the knife but inadvertently ended up pushing the knife forwards and it fell on the floor close to two ladies dining in the table next to them.

"I am so sorry," Ray apologized.

"No problem at all," one of the ladies replied as she picked up the knife for him. "You have a lot on your mind," she remarked.

Ray was surprised to hear this. Apparently, the two ladies had been overhearing the conversations of the three friends while they were waiting to order their meals and eat too.

"What did you mean?" Ray inquired, being very surprised at the lady's comment.

"We could not help overhearing your conversation. I am Nancy, and this is my twin sister, Stacy."

At this point, the twin sisters made eye contact with Kamal and Adam and exchanged greetings.

Nancy continued without being asked of her opinion. "I really feel for you guys, but there are some things that I would like you to consider."

Ray, Adam and Kamal were too dumbfounded to know what to say. They just looked on, mouth agape, wondering what would come next.

Nancy and Stacy were well dressed middle-aged ladies. They

were born in Greenbelt and attended Eleanor Roosevelt High School. Nancy is a Gynecologist and lives in San Francisco while Stacy still lives in Greenbelt and works for the Department of Education in Washington DC.

"I think it may be helpful if you try to understand what may be going on with your spouse rather than merely judging her actions. It may give you a better insight into what is going on and help your marriage," Stacy suggested.

She paused, but nobody spoke. So, she continued.

"Andy and I have been married for twenty-five years now and things are great. This was my second marriage. My first marriage lasted for only twenty-two months. Even though, we have known each other for about four years and had courted for three years prior to getting married. I felt as if I was put in a box after the marriage. It was terrible. I felt suffocated by him. It was horrible. It was as if his expectation in marriage was quite different from mine and we just couldn't make it work. So, we went our separate ways. I think you guys should try and get through to your wives. What they are going through that is influencing their decisions and behavior may not be very apparent to you. With Andy, I am more forthright in a respectful manner with whatever I feel and we communicate much better. Fortunately, that has worked well for us for a quarter of a century now."

"Well, I have talked to mine a billion times. It was like talking to a wall," Ray countered.

"Maybe you were speaking in a language that she did not quite understand," Nancy joked with a smile. "Seriously, please give your wife the opportunity to turn around. Think about it this way. Each of you is an individual in marriage. One and one can come together side by side and become two digits as eleven. This is the maximum a couple can get. However, it will only occur when there is nothing modifying their togetherness. If you put anything between them that defines or modifies their relationship, the outcome will be less than eleven. If you put a multiplication sign, the result is one. If you put a plus sign, the result will be two. However, if you put a negative sign between them, the result will be zero. Believe me, your wives don't want zero. Their actions may not make this obvious to you, but take my word for it. They will surely prefer their marriage to work and keep their families intact. So, care needs to be taken from both parties to avoid negativity between them. Try not to get mad at your wife. Mad, as spelled is M-A-D, which really stands for *Mutually Assured Destruction* which will not benefit you, your spouse, or your children."

Adam, Ray, and Kamal looked at one another with facial expressions which suggest their throwing their hands in the air.

"How do you reach a lady who doesn't want to talk to you?" Adam inquired.

"Try and use what she liked and enjoyed prior to the misunderstanding," Stacy suggested.

"I have tried cards, poems, chocolate and fancy restaurants but nothing worked," Ray resigned.

"Maybe try a direct talk. Ask her what she thinks you can do to make your relationship better," Nancy chimed in.

Then, the sisters wished the guys well and left.

Adam looked at Kamal and Ray and asked, "What do you guys think?"

"Well, they spoke from the perspectives of ladies. Maybe there are things we just did not understand as they pointed out," Kamal opined.

"I think it will help if women communicate rather than just nag," Ray suggested.

"Maybe they consider it as communication and we consider it as nagging," Adam explained.

"What I never could understand is when women expect you to know that something is wrong or that something is bothering them without telling you. It is as if they expect you to... just know," Ray wondered.

"For some women, a good partner must be a mind reader," Kamal offered.

"I had a moment like that with Desiree in the past. I had forgotten something that I promised to do. According to her, I was looking at her and she gave me the 'gaze' or the 'eyes' or something to let me know that something was wrong. Honestly, it was true that I was looking at her, but I was focusing on something else. You know, something really nice which I later wanted to touch, but she rebuffed me claiming that I was 'unbelievable.' They just make things very confusing. I feel it works better for everybody if our women will just communicate with us nicely. It will prevent us from forgetting things they consider important. This will also make us understand and be prepared for challenges when they arise," Ray concluded.

Part Three

Acting the Balancing Act: The Story of Adam

Part Three: Section One:
Sunset at Noon

Ray and Kamal looked at Adam wondering what has been going on with him. He had mentioned that his wife of thirteen years died three years ago. The expression on Adam's face was very indicative that he still misses his wife.

Kamal put his hand on Adam's shoulder and said, "Sorry for your loss, my man. Take heart. Everything will be okay."

Ray echoed the same support as Adam fought his tears.

"Eva was a lady of ladies," Adam remarked as he cleared his throat while cleaning his face with his handkerchief. "We also met in college."

Then, he chuckled and passed a comment, "It is funny that what happens in college doesn't stay in college." He then pointed an accusatory finger to his buddies asking a rhetorical question "Didn't your parents send you to college to get education, but you ended up chasing girls?"

"And what about you?" Ray retorted.

The three of them laughed together diffusing the pensive mood.

"Eva was a petite beauty. She was only five feet tall. I used to tell her that her five feet claim was rounding up from four feet eleven inches in heels. Her maximum weight that I know was a hundred and eighteen pounds when she was pregnant. She was really a great example of a precious wonderful thing that came in a small package. More precious than a diamond," Adam opined.

"Mmmmm!" Ray mused.

"We met when I was in my final year of medical school during my internal medicine rotation. She was a nursing student also rotating through the department of medicine for her clinical bedside experience. Simply put, she was the type of attractive nurse who would take an unreliable blood pressure measurement," Adam suggested.

"What do you mean?" Ray inquired

"There are some nurses that are so attractive that when they take the blood pressure of a man, his blood pressure will be high, and his heart rate will be fast, but when another nurse retakes the blood pressure and count the patient's pulse, they will be dead normal. This is what I call visual hyper-excitatory cardio-cerebral syndrome. In this condition, you become hyper excited about something you have seen that affects your heart and shuts down your brain into a non-intoxicated stupor," Adam explained.

"Wow!" Kamal responded

"Okay, that is a fake medical diagnosis. However, it aptly describes what we often see in the clinic. That is why if you see the blood pressure of a man that is elevated, you should repeat it before you label him as being hypertensive," Adam concluded.

"That is totally understandable," Ray agreed.

"I met Eva for the first time at the nursing station. Honestly, I forgot why I went there when I saw her. It was a temporary amnesia of some sort. What I remembered was that I must have developed high blood pressure myself. I had a rapidly beating heart that was heavy and heaving at the same time. My heart was galloping away like a Kentucky Derby horse on mega doses of steroids. I could only mutter a greeting and I left the nursing station. I was shocked to my bone marrow.

Over the next two weeks, I got to know her better. I was always very happy when she was assigned to my patients. I seized every opportunity to see her under the pretense of discussing my patients with her. She was an outstanding nightingale nurse. It is a shame that they don't make nurses like those anymore," Adam opined.

"What do you mean? Did something change in the nursing profession?" Ray inquired.

"Eva was a true nightingale nurse. It wasn't just because she had a fantastic soothing voice that will make nightingale birds jealous, but she embodied the honor, duty and care that make nursing a noble profession. A few decades ago, nurses wore uniforms which typically consisted of a starched white dress with a white cap. The student nurses wore pink dresses with white covered shoes to match to distinguish them from registered nurses. When you saw a nurse in those days, half of your illness was gone with how pleasant they were, how comforting they were, how empathetic they were, and how genuinely interested they were in your recovery. Nurses these days barely have enough time to know the names of their patients. It seems that documenting encounters is more paramount than the real interaction with the patients. I must say, this is true for medical doctors too. We are expected to see patients within five to fifteen minutes and document our clinical encounters. It is terrible."

"It is unfortunate," Kamal remarked.

"Unfortunately, things are likely to get worse in the humane part of medicine. The art of patient interaction seems to be buried in the annals of time. Technology is everything these days. Anyway, I was in the 5 North medical ward with Eva during our 4 weeks' rotation. She was very duteous, very respectful, very studious, and she had a wonderful personality. You could tell that her heart was really into helping people get better. We got closer and one day I mentioned to her that I liked the way she interacts with her patients and their families. She smiled. My brother, that was the most inviting smile I have ever seen. She thanked me for the comment and for my words of encouragement. The heaven really smiled on me the next day during the Attending teaching round. The student nurses and some registered nurses joined us for this round. The attending asked a lot of questions, and fortunately I was able to get all the questions correctly."

After the round, she smiled at me and remarked, "You do know your stuff."

I smiled back, being very happy, and remarked, "You motivated me to be the best that I can be too."

"I really don't know why, but this statement really touched her from the expression on her face. I saw a window of opportunity to express my feelings to her. At that point in time, I knew at least a medicine resident and a surgery resident who

171

had talked about their interest in asking her out. Hearing those guys made me jealous somehow. In any case, I knew that I had to make my move early to stand a chance. Therefore, after we had finished our clinical duties for the day, I went straight for the pick-up line that I had practiced."

"'Eva,' I called her name with an *I need something from you* tone and facial expression."

"Yes, Adam," she replied.

"I must confess that I get a tingling feeling in my precordium whenever I see you. The American College of Cardiology define it as love. The problem is that I am not sure if you will give me a chance because I have not achieved my life goals," I stated faking a serious look.

"And what are those goals?" Eva asked with a smile.

"I want to be six feet tall, handsome and rich. Right now, I think that I am zero for three," I replied.

"You are very funny," Eva responded.

"I am serious. However, if you are by my side, your essence will elate me and I will feel six feet tall and on top of the world. If you agree for us to be close, I will be very contented with what I have. In my heart, I will have the riches that men crave. Finally, if you choose me and touch me with your hands, I will be more than sixty percent handsome immediately."

"What did you mean by more than sixty percent handsome with the touch of my hands?" Eva asked, playing along.

"Because H-A-N-D-S are the first five letters of the eight-letter word H-A-N-D-S-O-M-E. Therefore, your hands will give me 'hands,' which is precisely 5/8, which is 62.5% of my handsome goal. I will only need to work on the remaining "O-M-E."

Eva could not control her laughter. She thought that I was funny. I read her a poem that I had written for her.

My Jewel of Inestimable Value
A lot of people died in search of gold
Many still endure hardship yet untold
Their souls have they sold
At least, that's what we've been told

People talk of diamond in the rough
Obviously, that does not apply to you

For you are polished and sparkling, yet tough
Bright, brilliant and beautiful. Yes, that's you

The best a man can get is a righteous wife
You personify everything I want in my wife
You are the joy of my life
You are the love of my life

Never have I seen someone so special, so clever
We will take good care of each other
And if you agree that we should be together
I will surely treasure you forever and Eva
I love you

"If Eva was trying to hide how she felt, the tears of joy rolling down her cheeks betrayed her.

I decided to hit the iron when it was still hot. I wanted to buy flowers and chocolate for Eva. However, I was so inexperienced, and I wasn't too sure whether to buy live flowers or plastic flowers. Surely, live flowers look brighter and you can smell them, but they attract insects and they die. Plastic flowers are somewhat cheaper from the dollar store and they stay the same, I reasoned. So, I bought a very colorful plastic flower and a card from the dollar store. I presented them to Eva with a pack of Hershey's kisses chocolate the following day. She was surprised by his gesture but was more surprised that I chose a plastic flower over a live one."

"On a curious note, may I ask why you thought that I would prefer a plastic flower over a live one?" Eva asked with a calm inquisitive voice.

"That was a great question. So, how did you respond?" Ray inquired.

Adam smiled and remarked, "I told her that just like my love for her, I want it to last forever. I do not want it to wither with the passage of time."

"Slick brother! You are real smooth operator," Ray acknowledged.

"Well, I couldn't tell her that I had no money or that I made a blunder," Adam defended his answer.

"I must admit, that was a great recovery. What did you write in the card," Kamal inquired.

My Beautiful Girl
She is the paragon of beauty
She is the S.I. unit of modesty
She is sweet, hot and tasty
She is meticulous; not hasty
She is nice and never nasty
She is my love and my reality

Eva,
You are the beauty of every beast
You are the focus of every masculine
You are the cynosure of every guy
You are the goal of every dude
You are the desire of every male
You are the dream of every man
You are the fantasy of every bachelor
You are the love of my life

"If she is really that great, what did she see in you?" Ray queried jokingly.

"Yeah, I agree. We need to query her judgment if she decided to go out with someone like you," Kamal agreed.

"My eyes, brothers, my eyes. They just have a knack for hypnotizing pretty ladies," Adam replied pretending to be very serious.

Adam continued, "We got married and things were great. We had two adorable children. Sheriff is my twelve-year-old son and Sarah is his nine-year-old sister. About six years ago, she was diagnosed with an aggressive triple negative breast cancer. Unfortunately, we never knew that cancer runs in her family because her people do not discuss their medical history. Apparently, her mother died of breast cancer at an early age. The story we heard was that she died during the childbirth of Eva's sister. The true story was that her mother was diagnosed with breast cancer when she was pregnant, and the disease progressed rapidly. She died soon after childbirth. Going through the ordeal of cancer treatment was tough on the family. What I found most deplorable and most appalling was the suggestion by one of the oncologists that if I had been a good lover, I should have felt the breast lump early enough. That was ridiculous, to say the least. Why will any husband be looking for breast lumps while in intimate moment with his wife? I was really upset, and we changed our oncologist. I really hope we can do more research to prevent all cancers and kick oncologists out of business."

Adam took a deep breath and continued, "Eva was thirty-six when she passed away in home hospice care three years ago. I was in total denial even after her burial. I was in shock for many a day."

I Am Waiting for You

I felt like dancing
But I couldn't
Because I wanted to dance with you
But you were not here

I felt like reading
But I didn't
Because I wanted to read to you
But you were not here

I felt like playing
But I wouldn't
Because I wanted to play with you
But you were not here

I have been waiting since last night
I waited all night
I waited all day in the sunlight
I am still waiting in this twilight

Another night is fast approaching
And I am still here waiting
Patiently waiting for you

"I am sorry for your loss," Ray comforted him.

"Thank you very much. It has been very tough for the children. I have been juggling my role and the role of their mother. People have advised me to remarry. It has just been difficult to move on. It has been tough to get Eva out of my head. However, I am seriously considering remarrying now," Adam related.

"That is an excellent decision, but what made you change your mind?" Kamal inquired.

"I realized that I needed to marry for myself and my children as well. It became more apparent a little over a year ago when Sarah, my younger child decided that she no longer wants to be taken to the boy's bathroom when we are in public places. I couldn't follow her into the ladies bathroom. Unfortunately, family style bathrooms are uncommon, and they are almost always occupied. Did you guys ever notice that when ladies go into bathrooms, it takes a long time for them to come out?" Adam asked.

"Yes, I know," Kamal replied. "Remember that I once did housekeeping job. It is because there are no urinals and the stalls are always never enough. So, they usually have long lines in the bathroom."

"Really? I did not know that. I have always thought that it is merely because they take too much time for everything. Then, they will reapply their make-up, making you wait endlessly for them. I have always opined that they just don't have any regard for a man's time," Ray expressed his long-held belief.

"Some of your opinion may be true, but this is also a simple building design problem that should be addressed. It is really tough to be waiting for my little girl to come out of the bathroom. It feels like eternity and of course, I cannot go in with her," Adam concluded in frustration.

"So, how is the search for a new flame coming?" Kamal asked.

"Dim. It is not going as well as I would have loved. I am having a difficult time choosing between the twenty-year-old lady I fell in love with and a thirty-nine-year-old divorcee who loves me," Adam blurted out.

Part Three: Section Two:
Is Love in the Heart or the Brain?

Love is an indescribable feeling!

W hy would you want to give yourself a premature heart attack by marrying a twenty-year old girl?" Kamal asked with a genuine surprise.

"Why not? She is a lady, not a minor. Besides, she is everything I ever wanted in my wife and I really love her," Adam explained.

"Is this all about midlife crisis? Do you feel like doing something dangerous to make you feel that you still have it as a macho man? If it is, why not just go buy a leather jacket? Or buy a crazy motorcycle or go bungee jumping or something? At least, these types of adrenaline rushes may break your leg, but they will not give you an emotional heartbreak that will kill you. This is what you are bound to get from this young girl. I know that you are a physician, so you know quite well that heart transplant does not fix heart attack and heart failure you get from a woman. Moreover, if my recollection is correct, you should be about forty-two years old now, right?" Kamal inquired.

"Yes. I am forty-two," Adam replied.

"So, you think it is a good idea to marry a lady who is less than half your age?" Kamal asked.

"She wouldn't be after two years. Furthermore, I truly love her," Adam explained.

"Don't mind the big guy. Tell me more about her," Ray interjected as he took a sip of his ginger ale.

Adam cleared his throat as if he was about to relate his odyssey to the land of love and excitement. The way he adjusted his position, any listener will be convinced that they are about to embark on the journey of love yet untold in the new world.

Kamal shook his head and remarked, "Oh boy! Midlife crisis at work."

Adam simply ignored him and continued. "It all started about ten months ago. The school sent a note to all parents of third grade students. We were informed that Ms. Paula Rossi had taken an extended leave of absence and that a substitute teacher, Ms. Nora Ahsan, would take her place. The note encouraged us to meet with the new teacher. Ms. Rossi had been teaching for over twenty years in the school. She was an outstanding teacher."

"Something major must have happened to the teacher," Ray opined.

"We later realized that Ms. Rossi had taken medical leave for a chronic illness and it was doubtful that she would return back to teach. In any case, after a couple weeks, I noticed that everything Sarah was mentioning was all about Nora, the new teacher," Adam continued.

"How so?" Ray inquired.

Kamal just shook his head being uninterested in the details.

"My daughter was always saying things like, 'Nora said sharing is caring,' 'Nora said don't shout at others,' 'Nora said say thank you to people,' 'Nora said greet people you meet with a smile, et cetera. It appeared that this new teacher seemed to have established a great bond with her. It was very obvious that she was enjoying school. You may not realize this, but it is not easy to be a single father. It has made me appreciate how much mothers really do for their children that men take for granted. So, I became more curious to meet this new teacher. On the day of the parent-teacher conference, I met her. I was shocked to see how young she was. I actually thought she was a teenager."

"Well, a twenty-year-old is a teenager plus one year," Kamal interjected.

Adam simply ignored him and continued. "It was very obvious that she is just a people person with an outstanding welcoming personality. She is easy to talk to and arguably one of the most cheerful people I have ever met. She is quite a dish too."

Kamal cleared his throat in jest.

"I must say that speaking with her for ten minutes about Sarah's education did not just make my day, it made my week. I was constantly thinking about this young teacher that I barely knew. She was just so special. I added one plus one and I got a billion. I mean, she is already her teacher; it will be a beneficial additional role for to be her stepmother too. I couldn't think of anything else. I started doing anything to get to know her better. I took time off work to volunteer in the school. I started doing anything the school needed parents to assist with. It gave me the opportunity to get to know her better. It worked like a charm. I learned that her mother also works as a teacher with Fairfax County Public School System. She taught second grade for many years and she is now the Vice Principal of Lincoln Way Elementary School in Falls Church, Virginia. Her father is a Computer Engineer and lectures at Potomac University in Washington DC. He is also a businessman and has a car dealership on New York Avenue in Washington DC. No doubt,

Nora has teaching genes in her genetic make-up. The best information I got from her was that she was born on October 5."

"And why is that important?" Kamal asked with skepticism.

"C'mon! That is the World Teachers' Day," Adam shouted with excitement. "It gave me the window of opportunity that I needed."

"Okay?" remarked Kamal.

"I had discussed with her previously that teachers don't usually get the praise they deserve for their hard work. Rather, they get criticized by parents who have failed their children and are often looking for someone else to blame. Thus, the poor teacher becomes an easy target of the parents' failures. I told her that I did not buy into the dumb statement that the rewards of teachers are in heaven. I argued that others have their rewards in heaven too. Think about it this way: will fire fighters who risk their lives battling wild fires to protect people and properties not get their rewards in heaven? Will police officers who respond to emergencies not get their rewards in heaven? Will water purification personnel not get their rewards in heaven? What about those construction workers who fix potholes on the roads in summer heat while they are being cursed by motorists who have been complaining that the roads have potholes? Surely, I think it is just fair that they get their reward in heaven too. So, getting reward in heaven does not mean that you should not get some reward here in the world. The only people that I do not believe should have any reward in heaven are lawyers."

"Hey! Watch it pal. Lawyers help the community too," Ray interjected.

"Yes, they help the community of criminals to escape justice," Adam countered.

"I know that you know better than that. Not all lawyers defend criminals. What about environmental and business lawyers?" Ray submitted.

"Well, those ones can get half reward in heaven, but divorce lawyers can go to hell," Kamal chimed in chuckling.

"In any case, I gave her a card for Teachers' Day when I dropped Sarah off in the morning. It was a poem with a subliminal message of engagement. I also informed her that I would like to see her briefly at closing time," Adam recalled.

The Wonderful Teacher
A teacher is a babysitter
It is not easy
To make babies sit in one place
A teacher is an instructor
It is not easy
To uphold and instruct goodness
A teacher is a role model
It is not easy
To do it very well

Seeing how wonderful you are
As a teacher
I am certain that you will even be better
As a mother

Thank you very much for all that you do

"When I saw her in the afternoon at school dismissal, she thanked me for the card. I had hoped that she would ask me what I meant by "I am certain that you will even be better as a mother." I was going to suggest to her that I am looking for a mother for Sarah. Unfortunately, she did not say anything about it. So, I hit a dead end with that move."

"An older and more matured lady would have understood your message," Kamal emphasized.

Adam did not behave as if he heard Kamal, he merely continued his narration of his encounter with Nora on World Teacher's Day and her birthday.

"Well, my alternate plan was still active for her birthday, so I gave her a birthday present which was a handwritten card with a poem and a box of exquisite Swiss chocolate."

The Verdict: Guilty or Not Guilty
You are accused of being very hot
Your hotness contributed to global warming
Yet, you are warm to those around you
Verdict: You are very guilty as charged

You are accused of being beautiful

181

Your beauty is deeper than your skin
Yet, your modesty is worthy of emulation
Verdict: You are wonderfully guilty as charged

You are accused of being very intelligent
Your I.Q. is beyond the scale
Yet, you are humble to all and sundry
Verdict: You are super guilty as charged

You are accused of being honest
Your morality reflects in your good character
Yet, you teach youngsters to be above board
Verdict: You are outstandingly guilty as charged

You are accused of being twenty-one today
Your look remains that of a sweet sixteen
Yet, your sense of maturity leaves us in awe
Verdict: You are exceptionally guilty as charged

You are hereby found guilty of all charges
You are hereby found guilty of being a wonderful person and
You are hereby sentenced to a life filled with happiness
Happy Birthday Nora!

"Nice!" Ray acknowledged.

"I know that I surprised her with the card and the gift. I really wanted to engage her a little bit more. I was thinking of taking her out on a date or something like that. However, I wasn't sure how to go about it," Adam regretted.

"Past your bedtime, old fella!" Kamal joked.

"I am not that old. Just a bit rusty. That's all," Adam countered.

"Somebody please get a walker. Old timer is on the move!" Kamal proclaimed while faking using a megaphone to make the announcement.

"I needed a simple way to get promoted from being a helpful parent to a darling husband. So, I volunteered in the school during my vacation. It gave me a lot opportunity to get to know Nora. The more I knew about her, the more I loved her," Adam recalled. There was a day I actually engaged her in conversation about her future career plans. I know that she is a very brilliant lady. She got her Bachelor's degree in three years and graduated summa cum laude. Even though I knew she enjoyed teaching, I was sure that she would prefer a higher level of education. I was not surprised at all when she mentioned that she would still like to go back to school. She informed me that she was thinking of a career in the healthcare field. Her top considerations included physical therapy, occupational therapy, nursing, and physician assistant career choices. When she mentioned physician assistant, I joked that I am a physician and she could be my assistant. That would make her a physician assistant."

"What did she say to that?" Kamal asked.

"She did not smile at all. So, I figured out immediately that it was a bad joke. So, I apologized and agreed with her that those were excellent choices. I had alternative career considerations for her in my mind though."

Your Career Choice

I would recommend criminology
This is a decision that may make you groggy
Given how swiftly you stole my heart
No doubt you will be a renowned expert

I would recommend pulmonology
This is a decision without an apology
Given how your beauty leaves me breathless
No doubt, the depth of my love for you is endless

I would recommend cardiology
This decision is due to my symptomatology
Given how seeing you makes my heart skip a beat
No doubt, your touch will treat my arrhythmia, a great feat

I would recommend rheumatology
This decision is real, not psychology
Given how your presence makes me perspire
No doubt, becoming your husband is my desire

I really really really love you

"Did you tell her this?" Ray inquired.

"No man. I couldn't. I developed cold feet. So, I kept it to myself. I still think it was a good poem though," Adam stated.

"As I told you before my friend, I really think that going after her was a bad idea," Kamal opined.

"Relax Kamal. Let's hear him out," Ray suggested.

Adam continued, "I knew that I had two cards, but I wasn't so sure which one would get me sympathy from Nora that will lead to love in her heart."

"What will those be?" Ray asked.

"I could play me as a suffering lonely nice guy who is badly in need of the help of a good lady for succor, or I could play the card of the poor motherless children who badly need a mother in their lives," Adam explained.

"So, which one did you play?" Ray asked

"I played both…"

"Let me guess," Kamal interjected. "They did not work."

"I wouldn't say that. There have been a lot of issues that have been difficult for me to understand," Adam related.

"How did you go about it?" Ray inquired.

"I actually scheduled an appointment with her, saying that I needed to talk to her. It was on a day that the school session was a half day. My intention was to take her to lunch, but I did not say so upfront for fear that she would turn me down. I was already in love with her and I could not really explain to myself why I loved her so much. It was an enigma. She is obviously very beautiful, but I know that my love for her is more than skin deep."

Reasoning for the Reason

I love you very much
But I don't know why
I care about you so much
But I am not sure why
I long for you too much
But I can't fathom why
I desire you very much
But I don't understand why
I look forward to seeing you so much
But I can't comprehend why

What I know
Is that my life has not been the same
Since I met you

All I know
Is that my life will not be the same
Without you

I love you.

"I did not want a rejection even though I knew that it was a very high possibility," Adam explained.

"I am glad that you recognized that your chances are poor. At least you have some insight," Kamal opined.

"My chance may be low, but it is not zero," Adam responded.

"Your chances are negligible. It is like one in… a million!" Kamal exclaimed laughing.

"I think you are wrong. That would suggest that there are a million handsome young men like me vying for her hand in marriage," Adam countered.

"Excuse me! Did you just include yourself in the handsome young men category," Kamal interjected.

"I never left that category, but I can't speak for you," Adam responded grinning.

"Ouch! That is below the belt," Ray chimed in laughing.

"C'mon man! You know that my chances are not that low given the number of men in the world and the ratio of men to women. However, even if my chance is really as low as one in a million, it is still better than the chance of winning the Powerball lottery which is one in two hundred and ninety million. So how many people do you think always invest their money in buying lottery tickets with very strong conviction and hope that they will win, Mr. Bookie?" Adam argued.

"Well, you are the doctor. I am just trying to save you from an avoidable emotional heart attack," Kamal alleged.

"Thank you for your concern, but she is the one I crave," Adam responded.

"I have made my point," Kamal submitted.

"And I have respectfully disagreed," Adam replied.

"Bravo guys! We have civility here," Ray proclaimed. "Can

we get on with the story please?"

"I really love this girl. She is a masterpiece," Adam related.

Masterpiece

She was created in the best mold
For all and sundry to astonishingly behold
She has a wonderful inviting stature
Bold, beautiful and attractive in nature
She is a masterpiece

Her physique is stunning and curvaceous
Her voice is melodious and mellifluous
Her smile is welcoming and infectious
Her walk is modest and gracious
Her hair is rich and gorgeous
Her skin is sensational and glamorous
Her front is eye-popping and fabulous
Her derriere is jaw-dropping and wondrous
She is a masterpiece

Baby, my assessment is real and meritorious
I am not joking and I am not being mischievous
She is my mind-blowing darling
She is a magnificent work of art
She is a masterpiece

Lucky me baby, lucky me!

"I decided to make my move," Adam recalled.

"So, you moved quickly on her? Scared that men who are also half your age will take her breath away?" Kamal teased Adam.

"Of course not! Well, maybe a little bit… but I have a lot of stuff going for me that they can't compete with too," Adam defended his candidacy.

"Really? Like what? Your brand-new walker or your new dentures?" Kamal asked in jest.

Adam punched Kamal on his left shoulder with his right fist. "You are underestimating the heart of a champion," Adam responded.

Adam related that he met Nora by the cafeteria after school

dismissal. She was as pretty as can be. She wore a faded blue denim shirt and yellow striped long skirt. She wore a left wrist bangle. Her purple lipstick was evenly applied on her luscious lips, that are tempting for a passionate kiss. As they walked past some paintings on the walls that were made by some students, he remarked that the paintings were made by future Picassos and Van Goghs. She agreed that some of the students were quite talented given their displayed work. His intention was to take Nora to the Tasty Choices Restaurant about a block from the school. He could not help giving her surreptitious glances under the false pretense of looking at the walls in the corridor. She was so graceful in her strides that Adam could only imagine how inviting she would be if she was actually catwalking. "My heart would explode," he mused to himself. She had the aura of an aristocrat as she descended the flight of stairs. He was breathless, but not out of climbing the stairs. It was from just looking at how beautiful she is. Her beauty took his breath away. She smelled so good, he had to caution himself not to ask her for a hug. He tried not to show how excited he was to be walking by her side. In his mind, he hoped that they would soon take a walk like this to the altar. "That would be awesome," he said to himself as he developed goose bumps.

As they walked out of the building, they noticed that it was drizzling. There was no hesitation on his part. He walked straight into the rain as if he needed the rain drops to cool him down, since her love made his core body temperature rise to seven hundred degrees Fahrenheit. For her, he felt that she needed the rain drops too to cool her down from being "too hot to handle." Walking next to her made him feel so elated, as if he was walking on water. Well, he literarily walked on water shortly thereafter. While he was busy glancing at her, he did not pay attention to the puddle in front of him and he stepped in it unwittingly. As the light rain fell on them, he looked at her face for the umpteenth time and some fell on her face. He looked at her eyes and they shone through like polished diamonds.

"It is great that we were not made from salt or sugar. We could have been melting slowly by now," Adam joked.

"True," Nora nodded in agreement.

Adam continued, "Although, if we were to be made from salt or sugar, I am pretty sure you will be made from sugar."

"What made you think so?" Nora asked stopping in her tracks.

"Because you are so sweet," Adam replied.

Nora chuckled.

The rain intensified a bit and he suggested that they should probably return to the school building. They both turned back, and he could not help glancing at her derriere. He loved everything he saw. She then asked him where they were going in the first place. He replied that he was taking her to the Tasty Choices restaurant for a bite and he could talk to her there as well. She smiled and thanked him but noted that she actually just had a submarine sandwich from Fresh Bake. They walked back to the large quadrangle in the reception area of the school entrance. The lobby was neat and beautiful. It had polished marble floor. The flags of the United States and the State of Virginia were conspicuously displayed. There were beautiful paintings hanging on the walls. The sun shone brightly at an angle into the lobby. An elegant chandelier hung on the cathedral ceiling. They sat on the comfortable green wicker chairs in the lobby with a beautiful green table with tempered glass surface between them. Adam looked at Nora and smiled. The only thing missing was a sweet-smelling love candle burning slowly to release love aroma in the air and complete the romantic setting.

Now is the moment of truth. He decided to tell her the truth. His heart started beating fast and his palms started sweating gently. He geared up to tell her about his love for her. He was not sure how she might react. Nonetheless, he could no longer suppress his feelings for her. He had been dealing with her love overflowing in his heart for too long. He has been constantly thinking about her. He longed to see her every minute. In the last one week, every time he looked in the mirror, he saw her face smiling at him.

Hallucination of Love

I see your smiling face everywhere
Some call this visual hallucination

I hear your sonorous voice all the time
Some call this auditory hallucination

I perceive your soft touch all the time

Some call this tactile hallucination

I feel your sweet presence all the time
Some call this love intoxication

All I can say is that
I love the feeling I get from you
Because you engage all my senses
In a unique way that
Only you can bring out the best in me.

I love you.

"Wow! You were hallucinating about this chick," Ray exclaimed.

"No. I was lovincinating. I must tell you though, it felt so good," Adam recalled.

"Pass the trans-fat! Heart attack is on the way," Kamal remarked.

"Anyway, I mustered the confidence and I related to her that I have deep-seated feelings for her. I told her that I have been having sleepless nights thinking about her. Furthermore, I informed her that the best view I have ever seen in Washington DC was during the ten-mile race of the Cherry Blossom at the peak of its bloom during the National Cherry Blossom Festival. It was a spectacular view at the Tidal Basin. I told her that she is the only person that I have ever seen in my life that struck me with more beauty than the cherry blossom," Adam recalled.

"Wow! That's deep," Ray concluded.

"It is true. I have fallen in love before, but it was never this strong. Definitely never to the point that my affection for the lady renders me paralyzed. I apologized to her if I came on too strong, but I pointed to my left ring finger to make a gesture to her that I would like to marry her. I really did not think there was any point beating about the bush. I reassured her that if she would give me a chance, being married would not affect her education. I promised to be with her all the way to achieve her dreams. Then, I asked her if she was mad at me for my proposal," Adam related.

"What did she say?" Kamal inquired.

"She said that she was not mad at me at all. That was a big

relief. Honestly, I was afraid that she may become upset, get up and possibly, even insult me. However, she did not appear surprised at all. It was as if she sensed what I was going to discuss with her. Her maturity in handling the situation further convinced me that she is the one."

She is The One
She is the one
She is the one for me.
She is the one I have been longing for.
She is the one I have been waiting for.

Her major comment was that she feels that she is still very young. I responded that she should take as much time as she needed to think about it, but that she is not too young to be married."

I am in Love with You
"Love is unpredictable," says the sage
"Love has no bounds," says an adage
But I know it is still a bit strange
Given our differences in age

The fact is that you've come of age
For your hand to be sought in marriage
Like a cherry blossom, you are at center stage
And my love for you cannot be gauged

Indeed, you have a superb image
My love for you is not a mirage
Let's show determination and courage
Let's pursue the path of marriage

Adam brought out a blank card and suggested to her that they fill the card together with whatever comes to their minds to commemorate their love conversation. She smiled, but responded with, "I am not going to say anything," which Adam promptly wrote down on the left side of the blank card.

"Now, it is my turn," Adam said. Then he wrote, "But I want you to tell me something."

Adam then motioned to Nora that it was her turn to say the next line. However, having realized that Adam was going to write whatever she said, she did not speak. Rather she motioned the fingers of her right hand over her mouth to indicate that her mouth is shut and she would not say anything.

"I have a lot of questions for you. Please answer them," Adam appealed to Nora as he started writing questions on the right side of the card which then read:

Questions Without Answers
It is as if
My world revolves around you
Why do I think the world of you so much?

It is as if
My living is really me and you
Why do I care about you so much?

It is as if
My life will be different without you
Why do I hold you dearly so much?

It is as if
My reality is being with you
Why do I long for you so much?

It is as if
My heart is with you
Why do I love you so much?

Sorry my love,
If I knew the answers
I wouldn't have asked you the questions.

I love you.

Although she did not want to speak, Nora was reading the message in the card as Adam was writing. When he finished writing "I love you," he could easily see tears well up in Nora's eyes. It appeared that something touched her heart.

191

The meeting lasted about an hour or so. It was the best hour that Adam ever had in his life as far he could remember. He felt on top of the world. He felt that a huge love burden had been lifted from his back. He was now anxiously waiting for her response. He gave Nora a card a few days later as a reminder of sorts that he was anxiously awaiting a positive response from her.

A Day to Remember
It was a great Friday
It was a wonderful day
It was a day like no other
It was when we got together

The meeting place was the cafeteria
Your radiant smile illuminated the area
You were a view so wonderful
You looked stunningly beautiful

When you were walking by my side
My profound happiness, I couldn't hide
We walked past the Sports Center
To be greeted by rain outside later

As we walked slowly in the rain
I couldn't help glancing at you again and again
We changed our minds about going outside
It was better to discuss inside
The lobby was quiet but elegant
The setting was simple, nothing extravagant

Today, all I want is for you to know
That my love for you is not a show
I truly love and care about you
And to me, there is nobody like you.
I love you.

"For the next five school days, my heart fluttered every time I dropped Sarah off at school hoping to see Nora. The following week, I was able to see Nora and I asked her for her response, she told me that she was still thinking about it. Honestly, I found it difficult to understand what was taking her so long to say yes. Then came the presidential election, her first. She was very happy to discharge this civic duty. I told her that she got my vote."

<u>You Got My Vote</u>

For the most beautiful lady in the world
I voted for you
For the most infectious smile
I voted for you
For the most caring heart
I voted for you
For the most illustrious spouse
I voted for you
For the most comforting partner
I voted for you
For the best companion a man can have
I voted for you
For the lady I want to be with forever
I voted for you

Sunshine,
Hope you had a blast
Voting in your first presidential election
Hope you will vote for me too
When the time comes for your selection
I love you.

"I really wanted to spend more time with her." Adam faced Ray and remarked, "Then it struck me. I remembered a time-tested strategy."

"What would that be?" Ray asked

"Always use what people consider to be important to get through to them. If you want to get through to a nurse, you should talk about taking care of the sick. If you want be a buddy to a chef, discuss an important recipe, and if you want to get through a teacher, education is the way to go. So, I came up with a suggestion for an educational field trip to the aquarium in Baltimore. It was a perfect plan," Adam related proudly.

"Tricky old man!" Kamal remarked.

"I convinced Nora that it would be a good educational experience for her to take her class to the Baltimore aquarium on a field trip. We got the students signed up. Of course, I volunteered to be a parent chaperon. My plan was simple. Two days before the trip, I went to the National Aquarium in Baltimore…"

"What for? You were going to be there in two days with the class anyway," Kamal questioned.

"And you are calling me an old timer. Who is out of the game now, young timer?" Adam responded.

"Okay! Just answer the question," Kamal replied.

"It was a simple preparation strategy. Going there a couple of days earlier gave me an opportunity to know the stuff there. That way, when we get there for the educational experience, I would not need to be studying the exhibits and displays. The students will be looking at the displays and the fishes, their teacher will be watching the students, and I will 'keeping an eye' on their teacher," Adam explained making air quotes with his fingers while saying that he would be keeping an eye on Nora.

"It will give me a good deal of time to spend with her. Hopefully, I can get my green light too. Yep, it was very simple. If they ask me any question, it will be unlikely to catch me off guard since I was just there, and they are highly unlikely to get new displays in two days. Pretty smart, isn't it?" Adam related proudly.

"So, how did the trip turn out?" Ray inquired.

"It was a disaster," Adam concluded shaking his head in disappointment.

Part Three: Section Three: Helping Buridan's Donkey

The trip to Baltimore was uneventful. I drove Nora and the twelve children in her class in a Ford transit passenger wagon I had rented. The journey was fun. The kids enjoyed themselves. National Aquarium is a modern educational treasure. The aquarium is near Baltimore's inner harbor. We got our tickets with ease and we took pictures at the entrance. If you have not been there, I highly recommend it for you and your children. It was a great experience from the first floor to the roof. We saw a lot of fish including sharks, stingrays, and fish that live at the bottom of the water and don't see sunlight at all. It was an eye opener for Nora. Fortunately, I came two days earlier, so I appeared very knowledgeable. The kids had a lot of fun touching the jelly fish under supervision of the attendants. We watched a 4-D film which was delightful. The children got enlightenment about the need for us to preserve the environment not just for ocean creatures, but for human beings as well. We had lunch in their cafeteria before we left," Adam recalled.

"It seemed you had a good trip. What was the disaster about it?" Ray queried.

"The disaster was about my interaction with Nora on our way back," Adam explained.

195

"What happened?" Ray questioned being very curious.

"We talked a lot about fish and the environment, but that was not really what I wanted to talk about. I wanted us to talk about us, but I just couldn't find the right words. Honestly, I wanted to get a 'yes' quickly, but I did not want to rush her. I was afraid that rushing her may make her say no. It was a fine line that I had to tread. So, when I realized that the kids were sleeping in the vehicle on our way back, I decided to broach the topic."

Fun lasts longer on water at Baltimore's inner harbor.

"How was the trip?" Adam recalled asking Nora.

"It was great. Thank you very much for everything," Nora replied.

"My pleasure," Adam responded.

After some moments of awkward silence, Adam spoke again.

"What about our conversation before Thanksgiving?" Adam mustered the confidence to ask Nora.

"I am still thinking about it," Nora responded.

"May I recommend a 'yes' decision?" Adam suggested with smile.

Nora smiled and turned her head to look outside the window on the passenger side of the vehicle.

Fish enjoy you watching them enjoying themselves at the Baltimore aquarium.

"Her smile melted my heart. I wanted her to continue talking. I mean talk about anything. I couldn't care. I just wanted her to speak to me, but she did not say anything. I should have just let the radio do the talking for both of us, but I got carried away with her presence and I started running my mouth as they say," Adam recalled with a true sense of remorse.

"What did you say?" Ray asked being very curious.

"Brother, what can I tell you other than that I was having verbal diarrhea," Adam stated rather dejectedly.

"C'mon! Tell us what happened," Ray pressured him.

"I started talking about my vision for us as a family including that I love her so much that we will have ten children," Adam recalled.

"Seriously? You told a twenty-year-old American woman that you wanted her to give birth to ten children for you?" Kamal jumped into the conversation.

"First of all, she is now twenty-one. Secondly, I was just joking. I just wanted to get her to say something," Adam explained.

"And what did she say?" Ray inquired.

"She responded exactly how Kamal responded. She said, 'Seriously?'" Adam answered. However, I was just too happy to be in her presence that I just continued to joke in my own little world. I replied rather unwisely saying, 'Of course, yes.' Then I told her that we will have a baby every year for the first six years and then every other year for four more babies to complete ten. I also started making up names that we were going to name our ten children. I felt so happy just talking to her. I think I lost it."

"No. I think you were just being yourself around her. If she did not understand it that way, then maybe she is not that matured yet," Ray opined.

"But what do you really expect? She is only twenty years—," Kamal stated but was interrupted by Adam who interjected saying, "Twenty-one."

"Okay, she is twenty-one. Are you happy now?" Kamal asked rhetorically and continued, "I know you like her but she—" but Adam interjected again saying "love her."

At that point, Kamal just gave up by throwing his hands in the air and turned his face away from Adam.

Ray looked at Adam and asked, "Did you tell her that you were joking?"

"Not exactly," Adam responded. "I actually continued to ramble on. I told her that we will get a six-bedroom house with a big compound. There will be no Ferrari for us. We will get ourselves an Airport Shuttle bus as our family vehicle. At this point, she was not saying anything anymore, but was just looking out of the window. She looked so beautiful. I think my brain stopped working."

"It is doubtful if it was working before," Kamal declared.

"Anyway, we got back to the school and I dropped them off. Nora turned to me after she got out of the vehicle and in a flat tone thanked me for the trip. She promptly turned and walked away. I started thinking that something was wrong, but I wasn't sure what to do. In the evening, I sent her a text message thanking her for making the trip possible and that I had a great time. Unfortunately, she did not reply. Over the next few days, I called her, but she did not pick up the phone and did not return my calls despite my messages. I made several attempts to talk to her in person, but it was obvious that she was avoiding me. I rewound the Baltimore trip in my head multiple times trying to decipher what went wrong. In the end, I thought that it must have been the talk about having ten children, but I wasn't certain. Nonetheless, I decided to send her a card with an apology."

Children by the Numbers

I am sorry for saying our children will number ten
I did not equate you to a hen
When I reduced the number to nine
I genuinely felt it was fine
When I said that we could shoot for eight
I actually thought that it will be great
Tell me, do you prefer seven?
If you say yes, then we are even
Please respond even if you prefer six
Your silence is leaving me in a fix
A really good number is five
For that, we can easily strive
We can actually go for four
We will get what we ask for
I know it is common to have three
Because it makes couples feel free
But there are those who have two
It does not mean they are not happy too
The truth is, we will be happy with one
So long as we remain together as one
I am so sorry my love.

"However, she still did not reply. I started shooting from the hip. I was a drowning man clutching at straw. Apparently, I had underestimated how much I loved her. My spirit was down. I lost interest in many things. I tried to see her and talk to her in private but I was not successful. I don't want to say that I became sad, but I was very, very, very unhappy."

Sunset in the Morning?

Last night, I was so sad and couldn't sleep
Yes, grown men don't cry and don't weep
But I really felt a deep sense of loss
That you chose to stay away, a great loss!

I really wish that I know why you are angry
I will be able to explain to you and say "I'm sorry"
Ignoring me may be your chosen way out
To me, it is a torture and I'm burning out

My love for you has given me a heartache
But your ignoring me is giving me a headache
This feels like an open wound, so deep, so raw
And I feel like a drowning man clutching at straws

Although I am currently black and blue
But no doubt, my love for you is true
It may be hard to say goodbye to yesterday
It is even harder to say goodbye to today

"She still did not reply to any of my text messages and did not return my phone calls. I did not want to give up, but my typical day was all messed up. I became desperate and I sent an email to her personal email address in an attempt to reach her. I was hoping that I would be able to get through to her heart."

<u>My Typical Day</u>
I wake up in the morning
I check my phone
To see if you have called

I go to freshen up for work
I check my phone again
To see if you've sent me a text message

I eat a quick breakfast of anything
So long as it tastes like something
I surely would prefer what you had
I drive to work thinking about you
I wonder how things are with you
I come home in the evening
I wonder how your day went

I go to bed at night missing you
I check my phone again
Hoping that you will call
I am very sorry.

"Although I was feeling heartbroken at this point, I was still holding on to hope. If only she could just tell me what annoyed her. If something else was going on, it was still better to share it with me rather than keeping silent. Her silence was killing me. It was painful. I mailed a card to her school."

Dancing in My Dreams

I know that you may not marry me
I am aware that we may not be meant to be
But you're the best damsel I've ever seen
And you're so lovely for beholders to see

Your goal is to be righteous
Your disposition is virtuous
Your smile is infectious
Your demeanor is gracious
Your character is auspicious
Your management is scrupulous
Your actions are judicious
And to me, you will forever be precious

To be with you remains my dream
You are the lady in my dream
I love you so much, I want to scream
Let's join hands and form a team
Let's come together and accomplish our dreams
I am very sorry for hurting your feelings
I love you.

"I got a note from Nora through Sarah a few days later. I am not sure what she really meant. However, I was happy that she said something at least. It simply read":

I am a Lady

I am a lady
Treat me like a lady
You are not my daddy
Treat me like a lady

A lady is not a malady
Treat me like a lady
I am not your baby caddy

201

I am a loving lady
Treat me like a lady

Adam asked, "What do you guys think she meant by *treat me like a lady?*"

"I can understand that she is not your baby caddy for your imaginary ten children, but I am also not sure what she meant by treat me like a lady," Kamal responded.

"Did you ask her for clarification?" Ray inquired.

"Of course, yes, but she did not respond," Adam replied.

"I still think maturity is still the issue here. She should know to just tell you what is going on," Kamal submitted.

"I still have no idea what she meant by *treat me like a lady*. I actually felt that I have always treated her with respect. I love her so much that I was even afraid that if she tells me to jump that I would ask how high. The last time I saw her was a week ago in Metropolitan Grocery, since school is no longer in session. I was so happy to see her. She wore a beautiful pink flowing gown, purple headgear, purple waist belt and was wearing a purple lipstick, her favorite color. Her pink gown had silver colored design at the edges. She looked as beautiful as ever. My heart melted again and her presence rekindled my love for her. I approached her and tried to start a conversation with her. Unfortunately, she didn't really want to talk to me. I told her that I was sorry about saying we will have ten children. She chuckled, making me realize that it may no longer be a big issue for her or that she had gotten over it. I kept on pressing her for what was going on, but she was unyielding with any information. Then out of desperation, because she started walking away, I asked, "Is it because of my age?"

Somehow, this made her stop dead in her track. She turned to face me and slowly walked back to where I was standing transfixed.

"What's age got to do with it?" She asked in a defiant tone. "My family is of the opinion that you will break my heart."

"I was shocked," Adam explained. I did not realize that she had informed her family. I tried to ask her who she told, but she did not answer my question.

"Nora! I would never break your heart. I know that you are very emotional, but I am very sensitive to your emotions," I tried to reassure her.

<u>Sensitive and Emotional</u>

You are emotional
I am sensitive
You are emotionally sensitive
I am sensitive emotionally
Do we have anything in common?
Yeah baby, we are complimentary.

Nora forced a smile and had a facial expression that conveyed an obvious message that she is confused about what to do in the situation she has found herself. Without saying a word thereafter, she lowered her gaze and she walked away leaving me in isle seven.

Kamal teased Adam saying, "Poor old man! You wanted to be with her on cloud seven, but she dumped you in isle seven."

Adam gnashed his teeth and clenched his fist, making Kamal move back in his seat.

"I cannot fathom what must have happened to my lovely lady that was making her avoid me. My intuition was to think that Nora talked to her mum. Maybe, she discouraged her. I don't know. Maybe she told her that I am too old for her or that I may break her heart or something. I don't know if the situation of her becoming a step mother to fairly grown children may also be a factor. Maybe some members of her family were making her feel that it will be a bad choice for her to be a stepmother at her age when she has just made it out of her own teenage years.

I really tried to find any reason that makes sense, but nothing did," Adam concluded.

"I am so sorry," Kamal stated on seeing the hurt displayed on Adam's face. "What are you planning to do now?" he asked Adam.

"I am not so sure," Adam responded sounding dejected.

"How about engaging her parents in discussion?" Ray suggested.

"She is not letting me through to them," Adam replied.

"What about trying your better candidate? I mean the mature lady that you are considering?" Kamal suggested.

"You mean Aneida?" Adam asked rhetorically.

"Aneida Newman?" Ray asked jokingly

"Yes. Did you know her?" Adam inquired being quite surprised.

"Not at all. I was just joking. You stated that her name is Aneida. It sounded like *I need a* that is why I added *new man*," Ray explained.

"Very funny, but her name is really Aneida Neumann," Adam informed them.

"So, how is she?" Kamal asked.

"She is okay," Adam responded.

"Just okay?" Kamal repeated.

"Well, what can I tell you?" Adam countered.

"Everything," Kamal responded.

"Well, Aneida is thirty-nine years old. She has been divorced for five years now. I was introduced to her by her cousin who is a nurse in our hospital about six months ago. We exchanged greetings a few times and we finally decided to meet about four months ago for lunch," Adam recalled. He then remained silent for some seconds which felt like eternity to Kamal.

"That's it? C'mon Adam, tell us more. Is it that her beauty did not measure up to what you are looking for?" Kamal suggested.

"No, it is not just about how beautiful she is," Adam replied.

"You know that she can still go to the labor ward at least four times with your babies. Maybe not quite the ten babies you wanted to squeeze out of Nora," Kamal asserted trying to sound very serious.

"You must be joking," Adam replied. "Pounding a thirty-nine-year-old lady with just one baby is the textbook definition of elderly abuse."

"Which textbook? That must be Adam's textbook of Priority Misplacement," Kamal countered.

"I am serious. When a woman is older than thirty-five years, her chance of having an abnormal or malformed baby such as Down's syndrome increases significantly. That is why it is important not to delay marriage unnecessarily," Adam explained.

"It is okay. I mean, you can be straight with us. We are guys too. We look at front yards and back yards too. All men are shallow, but some are just shallower than others," Kamal submitted.

"Seriously, it is not about how attractive she is. Of course, she is not on the same level as Nora, my lovely cherry blossom. However, when we met, she looked just the way she was in the picture that she sent me. She is at least honest and self-confident about how she looks. In any case, she asked me a lot of probing questions. I started wondering what this was all about. I mean, I was saying to myself that here is a thirty-nine year-old lady with two children. Her son, Ben, is fourteen years old and her daughter, Evelyn, is ten years old. She seemed very picky for somebody who is on rebound and not even in her prime," Adam continued.

"What did you mean by rebound?" Kamal inquired.

"She is trying to rebound from a failed marriage," Adam responded.

"I see. What an interesting description! So, tell me, was it offensive or defensive rebound?" Ray asked jokingly.

"Judging by the interview slash interrogation she gave me, I would definitely think of it as offensive rebound. She even subjected me to her so-called screening test."

"Screening test?" Kamal asked.

"Yes. Apparently, she developed her own analysis of men's behavior. She believes that it can make women determine what kind of man is good for them," Adam explained.

"And what is the screening test?" Ray asked being very curious.

"It is something like this. There were three men who were guests of a very rich man who lives in an outstanding luxurious estate while they were exchange students in the United States for four weeks. One day in their fourth week, the men were conversing with the rich man who had been a very gracious host for their entire stay. They asked if they could swim in his Olympic-size swimming pool. The man agreed and asked them to give him some time to ensure that the pool is ready. About thirty minutes later, he came back and informed them that the pool was ready. The first man went straight to the pool and jumped in with his street clothes. The second man went to his room to change his clothes into his swimming gear and then left for the swimming pool. The third man went to the swimming pool to check if the pool was really ready. Then, he stuck his foot in the pool in order to confirm that everything was okay and the temperature was perfect. Are you more of the first, the second, or the third man?"

"That is a good one. So, what type are you?" Kamal asked.

"I will tell you, but what type do you think you are in this analogy?"

"Given how badly Kandie treated me, I will want to be the third guy. Never trust anybody no matter how good they may appear to be. However, given how wonderful Bonita has been as Kandie's replacement in my life, I am still trusting. So, I am definitely the second guy," Kamal answered.

"I agree with you. I am the second guy too. I would have known this host and lived in his house for about four weeks. I will probably trust his judgment. I will go and change and go to the pool too," Adam responded.

"What type of men did she think the other two were?" Ray asked.

"I did not ask her. But my take is that the first man is a happy-go-lucky person. He will be ideal for any woman who is looking for a spontaneous explorer who lives on the edge. He is more of an act first, think later man. The third guy trusts no one," Adam opined.

"Was she satisfied with your answer?" Kamal asked.

"I guess so, because we started talking into better details afterwards. I think she was just trying to avoid what happened with her former husband," Adam explained.

"I supposed that she had a really bad experience," Ray chimed in.

"Well, I really did not ask for details. However, she mentioned that the guy's name is Phillip. Sometimes, she will refer to him as Phillip the flip flop. She said that he was very nice and very spontaneous when they started dating. He had quick wits, and was very funny. He said that the guy could improvise within a blink of an eye. She gave me an example that one day he was working in an 'Ask me' station during the convention of a national organization in Walter E Washington Convention Center in Washington DC. Some college students came to the booth to play a prank by asking him a question that they felt would rattle him," Adam related.

"What did they ask him?" Ray inquired.

"One of them asked him, 'How can I become a millionaire?' They were surprised when he answered them spontaneously with a straight face, 'Just have a million dollars and you are automatically a millionaire.' So, the joke was on them," Adam related.

"Sounds like an interesting guy. What then crashed their marriage?" Kamal inquired.

"I do not know the details. It seemed that there were many

issues. I think he lost his customer service job and had difficulties finding another one that could match what he was doing before. Unfortunately, he started running with the wrong crew. He tried his hands on many jobs including selling used cars and driving taxi cabs but didn't quite make it. According to Aneida, he constantly told her lies too."

The Pathological Liar

He said his eyes are blue
But that's when he wears contact lenses
He said his hair is black
But that was after dying it
He said his teeth are white
But he did not mention that they are dentures
He boasted that he has money in the bank
He did not say that it was a paltry twenty dollars

"He started trying to comfort himself with the bottle while hoping to hit the jackpot on the gambling scene. This made things harder for the family and their marriage started falling apart. Aneida works as a respiratory therapist in a long term acute care facility in Maryland. She said that she had to work two jobs, yet Phillip will come home drunk. He started smoking cigarettes at thirty-four years of age. "Who picks up smoking at thirty-four?" she asked rhetorically. She said she tried to get him to quit but that never happened. She emphasized how traumatic it was for her as a respiratory therapist with all she sees at work to now have a husband who smokes. It was really depressing for her. He had no money to pay any bill. She said that she tried to keep her marriage until it was too obvious that he was becoming a bad influence and she did not want him around the children. Hence, their divorce."

If Only

If only we eat weeds
We won't mind them in our lawn
If only rats pay rent
We won't mind them as co-tenants
If only mosquitoes don't bite
We won't mind their buzzing music

> If only flies don't transmit diseases
> We won't mind their display on food
> If only roaches lay golden eggs
> We won't mind them in the kitchen
> If only he is great between the sheets
> I won't mind that he is very poor

"Ouch! That is so depressing. At least now we know why she called him flip flop. The flip is in his career and behavior while the flop is in the important department," Ray joked.

"That is what some of these bad habits do to you, especially cigarette smoking. It is not just cancer and heart disease they cause, but they also make you lose your lady's respect too. We had a urologist give us a lecture in our Medical Grand Rounds a few years ago. He told us that men who smoke have to make up their minds about where they want their breathlessness to come from. They can get breathless from lung diseases such as emphysema or chronic bronchitis from smoking or from dancing to silent drums between the sheets with their wives, but not both," Adam recalled.

"At least, both of you have clean slates. So, did you guys hit it off from zero to sixty miles an hour in one second?" Ray joked.

"I don't know anything about that," Adam replied.

"So, when are you guys getting married?" Kamal inquired.

"Am I supposed to be laughing? That sounds like a horrible joke," Adam retorted.

"C'mon! Relax. She can't be that bad," Kamal responded.

"I am not saying that she is bad. It is just that my heart is with Nora," Adam responded in a dejected tone.

"My friend, you need to snap out of it. You are like a hungry guy under an apple tree. He wants to pluck an apple from the tree by himself, but he has no ladder and does not know how to climb. Yet, he is refusing to take any apple that fell by itself. Are you planning to die of starvation?" Kamal asked rhetorically.

"Nora or Aneida? That is the question," Ray broke the decision down.

"Definitely Aneida. No comparison," Kamal opined.

"I don't care. Choose the lady who will make you her priority and take care of you. In the end, if the speed limit is forty miles an hour, it does not matter whether you drive Lamborghini Veneno, Ferrari Pininfarina, or Kia Rio, so long as you get to your destination," Ray submitted.

"It is not about going from point A to point B, or traveling at the speed limit. It is about the experience of the journey. If you have a Lamborghini in your garage, you may feel more fulfilled driving it and you may drive it more," Adam countered.

"That is your assumption. Have you ever seen a Lamborghini for sale with a mileage over a hundred thousand before? These types of cars are only for show. They are not the day-to-day work horse that men like us need. On the other hand, a Toyota Corolla may have over two hundred thousand miles under its belt and it is still kicking well," Kamal argued.

"Enough of car parables! All I know is that I am in love with Nora. As per Aneida, I am not so sure," Adam explained.

"I think you are trying to make this very important decision with your heart rather than your brain. It is obvious that Aneida is the better choice for you at this point," Kamal opined as he placed his hand on Adam's left shoulder. "You need somebody like Aneida for your children. She has the experience and her children and will provide a better network for your children too. It is very straightforward," Kamal insisted.

"I get that. I understand. She will take care of our combined children, but what about me? What about my needs?" Adam questioned.

"She will take care of that too. It is not that she is too old," Kamal responded.

"No, she is old. At thirty-nine? C'mon man! She is very old," Adam disagreed.

"I do not understand this. Aneida is exactly the same age as Eva. I am sure that if Eva was here, you would not be regarding her as old," Kamal reminded Adam.

"That is true for age, but I only see Eva for what she was when we met back in college. As per Aneida, she is old. End of story," Adam reaffirmed his position.

"Masculine hypocrisy at its very best! What is wrong with you guys? She is three years younger than you and you are calling her old! What does that make you?" Kamal argued.

"Of course, mature. You can't compare the aging process of a man with that of a woman. I am like cheddar cheese, aging gracefully with an increasing intense flavor. However, she is like milk, you want her fresh with all the nutrients," Adam counter argued while laughing.

"You are just wallowing in self-deceit. If you marry this extra young babe, your problems will go from ninety-nine to two hundred," Kamal predicted.

"You can't be serious!" Adam rejected this wrong prediction. "You are trying to make it sound as if she will be bringing one hundred and one problems to my life. I love her, and I am happy whenever I see her."

"Make the decision with your brain my friend, not your heart. If you let this chick break your heart, nobody will be able to 'un-break your heart' for you. You know as well as I do that Aneida is your better choice," Kamal concluded.

<u>Your Better Choice</u>
Your need someone with experience
She has acquired experience
You need someone with patience
She has acquired patience

Just because she is old
Does not mean she is cold
Be bold my friend, be bold
Deep down, you know she is gold

"Believe me, I may have more calendar years, but I have more activities left in me than she has left in her. Maybe in two years, she will tell me that she is through with dancing between the sheets, who knows?" Adam asked with a genuine concerned look.

"Who knows if you will be the first one to go soft? Then you will need the little blue pill to help you get to wonderland," Kamal countered.

"You can say whatever you want," Adam submitted.

"Listen my friend, if you chose Nora, what if she is not yet mentally mature enough to be a mother to Sheriff, your twelve-year-old son? Moreover, she has been turning down your love proposal anyway," Kamal reminded Adam.

"I don't think her saying 'No' means that she is really turning me down. I think she is just struggling with 'Yes' as the answer to my proposal. However, I am very optimistic that she will soon come around," Adam rationalized.

"Oh my God! This is the textbook definition of self-deceit," Kamal expressed his opinion.

"My friend, pick the lady who will take care of your needs. Whether she is young or extra young, it does not matter at all if she does not do her part to bring comfort to your life," Ray concluded.

"What I need to figure out is the conundrum with Nora. Does her saying no mean that she really wants me to leave her alone or is she trying to tell me to try harder? I wish Nancy and Stacy were still here so that we could ask them for their opinions," Adam submitted.

(**Author's note:** How can you differentiate a hard chase from harassment? How can a guy who is in love know that a "no" means "end of the road" versus "try harder"?)

If only Adam has a vintage point view similar to looking at Washington DC from the top of the Washington Monument.

Epilogue

The gentlemen finished their meals and gave one another a firm handshake wishing one another the very best in dealing with their marital challenges. Then, they left the restaurant and headed to their homes.

After about thirty minutes of driving and trying to process all the discussions he had with Kamal and Adam, Ray started wondering what he could do to geth through to Desiree. He cannot afford to give up, but he needs her to treat him well. He started humming to himself:

<u>Treat Me Well</u>
Treat me well Desiree
Treat me well Desiree
I will do the same for you
Treat me well Desiree
Treat me well Desiree
I have always been nice to you

Treat me well Desiree
Treat me well Desiree
There's no one in my life but you
Treat me well Desiree
Treat me well Desiree
I don't want anybody else but you

Treat me well Desiree
Treat me well Desiree
I have opened my heart to you
Treat me well Desiree
Treat me well Desiree
My heart is pumping hard for you

Treat me well Desiree
Treat me well Desiree
I have a lot of love for you
Treat me well Desiree
Treat me well Desiree
I will give all my love to you

Treat me well Desiree
Treat me well Desiree
I will give everything I have to you
Treat me well Desiree
Treat me well Desiree
All I want is to be with you

Ray decided to give his marriage to Desiree a chance to rejuvenate. He made a detour and headed to the neighborhood supermarket to get a bouquet of roses for Desiree hoping for a fresh start. Suddenly Ray's phone rang. It was Desiree.

"Could you please get some fresh tomatoes on your way back?" she asked.

"Have you finished cooking?" he asked her.

"No. I have not started preparing the food," Desiree replied.

"I will get the tomatoes, but I am thinking of giving you a break. Would you like me to get us some Chinese food?" Ray asked.

"That would be wonderful, my dear," Desiree replied.

Ray froze. Desiree had not called him "my dear" in over two years. He got goose bumps. Maybe things will get better after all. He became more hopeful than ever.

"I love Hunan shrimp," Desiree informed him.

"Me too, darling," Ray responded. "I will get some Chinese food on my way."

"Alright. I will be expecting you home soon," Desiree

concluded sounding happy.

Kamal got home and as usual, Bonita met him at the door looking so beautiful, gorgeous and angelic. Kamal hugged her very tight and whispered in her left ear as her beautiful emerald earring swung back and forth like a pendulum, "I love you and nothing can change that."

Bonita then asked, "Thanks, I love you too, but did something happen?"

"Nothing. I just appreciate more and more how lucky I am to have you as my wife," Kamal replied.

"Aww, baby. Me too," Bonita replied as they shared a passionate kiss.

Kamal's heart was beating so fast while he was trying to convince himself that he told her the truth and did not really tell a lie.

Adam got home and put on his laptop computer. He tried to convince himself not to look at Nora's pictures. However, he was unsuccessful, and he looked at her pictures on Facebook and Instagram for the umpteenth time. He realized that he still really loves her. He decided to send her an email. "Nora my love, I hope you are having a great day. Smile and rejoice. Sing and rejoice, for you have a great voice. Smile and rejoice. I hope you'll make me your choice. I love you very much and your love shocks me like electricity."

Electricity
Nobody else charges me for love
From cathode to anode
For you activate my sinoatrial node

Nobody else makes my day full of love
From morning to evening
For you always make fun everlasting

Nobody else packs my night with love

217

From night to day
For you make my day, today and everyday

Nobody else quenches my thirst for love
From the land to the sea
For you are the joy that I see

Nobody else satisfies my hunger for love
From the hills to the valleys
For you are truly a lily of the valley

Nobody else has enduring season of love
From summer to winter
For you run in my mind like a sprinter

Nobody else fills me with love
From the East to the West
For you are simply the best

I love you and
I miss you so much

About one hour later, he got a reply from Nora that simply read, "Do not try to contact me or speak to me again. I've tried to ignore it, but this is too much. Leave me alone. If you keep bothering me, I will…"

Adam wondered what Nora was going to do? What is she trying to threaten him with? Was it a crime to love her?

A part of him felt that Nora was rude, but the love in his heart made him decide to overlook her fault. He composed a response to her.

<u>Yes and No</u>
It is okay
Not to love me

But

It is not okay
To be mad at me

For loving you

It is very hard for me
To hide my love for you
It is impossible for me
To suppress my love for you
It is not feasible for me
To ignore my love for you
It is unachievable for me
To erase my love for you

I just can't help it.
I am so sorry for it.

While he was proofreading the email, his phone rang. It was from Aneida. He ignored it and let it go to his voice mail. He continued to proofread the email message he was planning to send to Nora. Just before he could hit the send button, his phone rang again. It was Aneida again. He did not pick up. However, Aneida did not leave a message this time around. Rather, she called back almost immediately. Adam convinced himself that this must be something urgent. So, he forced himself to pick the phone.

"Hello, Aneida," he said in a soft voice, trying to sound as if he was tired or was just waking up from sleep.

"I am great," Aneida replied sounding very excited.

"Did you win a billion dollar from lottery?" Adam asked being sarcastic.

"Something better," she replied.

"Interesting! What is it?" Adam asked her.

Aneida exclaimed with excitement "My parents are coming to town tomorrow morning for a reunion and they want us to have dinner with them tomorrow."

Adam pressed the mute button on his phone so that he can express himself without Aneida hearing him.

After a few seconds, Aneida's voice came through the phone again saying, "Hello! Hello! Adam, are you still there? Will you be able to make it?"

THE END OF BOOK 1

ABOUT THE AUTHOR

Dr. Adeyinka O. Laiyemo, MD, MPH, is an Associate Professor of Medicine. He is a gastroenterologist and practices medicine in the District of Columbia. However, his heart is in art. He has done a lot of literary work as a featured writer for The Daily Champion in Nigeria in the 90s. His poems have been published in anthologies in the United States.

Adeyinka loves comedy, poetry, and enjoys traveling. He is currently working on episode two of the trilogy entitled: *Three Guys Talking 2: When Ladies Fight Back*.

blissfulgardenz.com

SPOILER ALERT

Do not turn the page if you do not want to have an idea what is coming in episode 2. The novel is entitled *Three Guys Talking 2: When Ladies Fight Back*.

Three Guys Talking 2:
When Ladies Fight Back

Thank you for your interest in this second episode of the trilogy "Three Guys Talking," a romantic seriocomic chronicle of the love life of Ray Marshall, Kamal Brown and Adam Gray from their points of view.

They had discussed their problems. Ray was lonely in his marriage as his wife has ignored him and mainly attended to the needs of their children. Kamal's happy marriage to Bonita is being threatened by Kandie, his ex-wife and mother of his only child who is trying to win him back. Adam, the forty-two year old widower is in love with Nora, now a twenty-one year old hottie who has been rejecting his love proposal while Aneida, the thirty nine year old divorcee who can be a mother for his two children wanted them to tie the nuptial knot. The friends proffered solutions for one another. The plans were simple, direct and practical. Unfortunately, human beings are too complicated.

Ray was supposed to woo Desiree, his wife of thirteen years, by being extra nice to her, assist her with house chores, bond better with his children, lose some weight and exercise more in order to be physically fit. This was suggested to bring back the good old days and prevent his marriage from going off the cliff. This worked perfectly until Desiree became pregnant again.

Kamal was to recruit Bonita as his quasi bodyguard. This will be his "temptation preventing strategy" against Kandie who is determined to wrestle him away from her. The problem was that there was no red line that Kandie was not prepared to cross to achieve her objective.

Adam did not feel choosing a wife should be this complicated. Yes, there should not be a big deal about him being in love with his twenty-one year old soul mate. The additional obstacle was that Nora's mother, who is his age mate, described him as "feverishly fighting furiously for a forbidden fantasy."

The stakes have only gotten higher, the challenges have only become more compounded and the task ahead has only become more difficult for the three friends.